KORIMAKO

KORIMAKO

David Nelson

Library of Congress Control Number:		2010917861
ISBN:	Hardcover	978-1-4568-1335-2
	Softcover	978-1-4568-1334-5
	Ebook	978-1-4568-0639-2

This book was printed in the United States of America.

To order additional copies of this book, contact:
Xlibris Corporation
0800-891-366
www.xlibris.co.nz
Orders@xlibris.co.nz
700082

DEDICATION

To Glen, Andrew, Sarah and Mike, who inspire me.

GLOSSARY

e noho ra	—	stay well
haere mai	—	welcome
haere ra	—	farewell
haka	—	posture dance (often used as a form of challenge)
hongi	—	press noses (a form of greeting)
iwi	—	tribe
pa	—	stockaded village
ka kite	—	see you
ka pai	—	very good
kapa haka	—	traditional performing arts
karakia	—	prayer
karanga	—	call (often used as part of a welcome)
kaumatua	—	elder
ki a koutou katoa	—	welcome to you all
kia ora	—	hello, or thanks
korimako	—	bellbird
mana	—	respect
marae	—	meeting place, focal point of a settlement
morena	—	good morning
noho rangimairei	—	stay in peace
pakeha	—	non-Maori person
rangatira	—	chief
tangi	—	period of mourning
tena koe	—	greetings to you
tena koutou	—	greetings
tena koutou katoa	—	greetings to you all
whakama	—	loss of mana
whakapapa	—	geneology, family tree
whanau	—	family

Prologue

Mike Robinson's last day at his Richmond home was another necessary step in the grieving process and he hoped his departure from a house that held so many poignant memories of the joy and love he had shared with Rosie would allow him to move on with his life.

For the last two months every day had been an emotional upheaval. Every day Mike had been reminded, so many times, of his beloved Rosie. The house still seemed full of her, but she was not there. It wasn't just the photographs, or the vases she always had filled with flowers, or the bed which still seemed to carry her scent, or her clothes in the wardrobe; it was everything about the home they had made together. Together they had decided how this house should be built, how they should decorate and furnish it, and how they should set out and plant their garden. Together they had turned a bare plot of land into a wonderful place for their family to live. They had been supremely happy here. Now, there was nothing in the property that didn't constantly remind Mike of Rosie.

Thinking things over, Mike had come to the conclusion that he would have to leave to give himself the chance to move on. It was not that he wanted to forget about Rosie, he would never forget her, but he recognised that the constant reminders, every way he turned, made him long so much for all that was now inevitably lost and in his past. Whilst he still grieved for Rosie, and so badly missed her touch, her smile, her warmth, her empathy, her intellect, her humour and her love, he couldn't think ahead to plan some kind of future for himself. At sixty-three years of age, and only recently retired from his engineering consultancy work, Mike knew he had to find a new purpose to his life. He had to shrug off the grief and misery he had felt every single day since he was told of Rosie's accidental death. He realised he had to leave and start again somewhere else; but what would he do then? He hoped he had at least twenty years ahead of him, maybe more than that if he was lucky, but he knew that keeping reasonably fit and well would only happen if he had something worthwhile to live for, some meaningful mental and physical stimulation, some way of filling the void that losing Rosie had created.

* * * * *

The furniture removal people had just left with a large truck-load of possessions. Mike had asked them to take almost everything to the auction house. His new start would include setting up a new household from scratch. He was only going to take his personal things: his office desk and chair, his paints and easels, his computer equipment, and his woodworking and gardening tools. These he had packed into his car, or had secured onto his trailer.

Mike took a last walk through the house and the garden, and looked up at the hills and across the township to the Waimea Estuary and Tasman Bay. It was such a beautiful place and it invoked such wonderful memories. He wondered if the people who had bought the place, and would be moving in tomorrow, would be happy. Of course they would. They couldn't fail to love the place the way he and Rosie had. Their young children would fill the house with noise and laughter, just as Paul and Julia had done before they had become young adults, moved to Christchurch to study for their degrees, and then made their careers abroad.

Finally, as he reached his car, Mike found himself completely choked with emotion. It was so hard to leave and tears ran freely down his face. He got into the car and took some deep breaths to calm himself. Then, with a last sigh, he turned the ignition key and released the brake. Without looking back he drove onto the road and away . . . In two hours he would arrive at Puponga and begin the next phase of his life; whatever that was going to be.

CHAPTER 1.

January 2008

When Mike told Paul and Julia that he was moving out of the house at Richmond they understood it was something he needed to do to deal with his grief. But when he told them he was moving to the caravan, on the two-acre block of land he had bought years before as a place for weekend retreats, they thought he was running away from his life. They couldn't see how a life of seclusion in a caravan, in such a small and isolated place as Puponga, could help him to overcome his loss. They hoped his decision to go there was some kind of aberration and would only be temporary.

* * * * *

Going to Puponga is like going back in time, thirty years at least. There is a camping ground with back-packer accommodation and about twenty houses, most of them hidden amongst kanuka trees. Less than half of them are used as permanent residences. The rest are simply holiday homes, used only occasionally. There are no footpaths, no shops, no garage, and no pub. There is an electricity supply and a weekly rubbish collection, but no water supply, or sewage system. On any weekday you will be lucky to see more than a handful of local residents, mostly older folk, checking out the flotsam on the beach, or doing some gardening. Sometimes you can go the whole day without seeing anyone, except in an occasional car driving past. Most people who venture to this north-west corner of the South Island are there to visit Farewell Spit and experience the wild beauty of Wharariki Beach, but only a few opt for an overnight stay at the local camping ground.

During his first voyage of exploration to New Zealand, in 1770, Captain Cook decided that the cape at the north-western tip of South Island should be named Cape Farewell. Just to the north of the cape a long finger of low sand-dunes forms a unique protective barrier between Golden Bay and the Tasman Sea. With its toi toi grass, flax, lupin and marram grass it curves eastwards for just over twenty kilometres. The Maori name for the spit is Onetahua, but it is commonly known as Farewell Spit. Golden Bay, which the

Maori knew as Mohua, is shallow and the tide can retreat up to six kilometres from the inside of the spit, exposing ten thousand hectares of mudflats. This creates a major hazard for migrating whales, especially pilot whales. Almost every year many become stranded on the spit as they try to navigate their way out of the bay and are caught by the change of tide. Once this happens their fate is often sealed. They will almost certainly die unless they are discovered quickly and the whale recovery team, with its numerous volunteers, is urgently assembled to keep them calm and moist, and to refloat and direct them to deep water at the next high tide. Inevitably, though, many succumb despite the valiant efforts of the rescuers.

Puponga's isolation and raw beauty gives it a special appeal all of its own. The tiny settlement is nestled in an inlet at the base of Farewell Spit and sits alongside Puponga Point, a lumpy peninsular that juts out into Golden Bay, and a large estuary that fills and empties with each change of tide. Lying just off the point a small, rocky island is favoured by seals and shags as a resting place after a long day at sea. From Puponga Point the inlet sweeps southwards. The beach is almost non-existent when the tide is at its peak and, if the wind is blowing, waves will surge to pound the rocks that have been placed along the high tide mark to protect the adjoining road. At low tide the sea retreats for eight hundred metres, leaving bare vast expanses of sea grass and mud flats.

Local fishermen can launch their small fishing craft at the outlet of the estuary and motor out past the peninsular, via a buoyed channel, to the sea. Snapper is the fish they most hope to catch, but kahawai is more plentiful. If the fish aren't running and the tide is out it is easy to walk out onto the exposed mud flats to dig for cockles. A bucketful will only take minutes to collect. At night, spear-fishing in the shallows can provide a delicious meal of flounder.

Long ago Puponga was home for a Maori tribe. The tribe built a fortified pa on the peninsular so that they could defend themselves when their enemies sent raiding parties to take women and slaves. Nowadays the pa site has become somewhat overgrown, but the form of terraces and ditches, carved out by the original occupants, can still be seen. Shell mounds, or middens, are also discernable.

The Maori people eventually moved away when much of their land was acquired by early European settlers. In the 1800's coal was discovered in the local hills and Puponga became a small coal-mining town. Two separate mines were worked, with tunnels being dug into the hills. Railway tracks were built to run from the mines to the waterfront and out along a wharf. In its coal mining heyday Puponga had two wharfs, one for each mine. The longest of these ran out into the bay for nearly a kilometre to clear the low tide mark. The coal was delivered to the wharves in small rail wagons. Flat-bottom scows, notably the Pearl Kasper and The Portland would then carry the coal to Nelson. Puponga was a busy community then, but the coal had been worked out by 1974 and now it has become just a small dot on the map. Most New Zealanders don't even know it exists.

* * * * *

Mike's two acres of land rises up from the road that runs along the beachfront. From his front boundary there is just a twenty metre road-width to the beach. Ninety percent of his land is thickly covered in native bush, mostly manuka, kanuka, karaka and whiteywood trees, and a variety of ferns and flaxes. Near the roadside, where the ground is low lying and a little swampy, tall stands of toi toi and harakeke flax flourish and shield the only grassed area from the on-shore winds and from the view of people passing by. This is a relatively flat space, but then the land suddenly steps up by seven metres; an escarpment formed by generations of erosion, caused by wind and rain. Beyond the escarpment the land rises, gradually, to a height of sixty metres above sea level.

From the road, access to the land is via an old wooden farm gate. A pebbled track leads to a caravan and an old shed, both sitting to one side of the grassy glade and tucked in behind the toi toi and flax, and sitting to one side of the grassy glade. The glade is sheltered from prevailing southerly winds by mature kanuka trees.

One of the things Mike loves best about Puponga is the birdlife. He can spend hours watching land and seabirds. When the tide is in, and he looks across the road to the sea, he can see gannets and terns diving to catch mackerel and other small baitfish. When the tide is receding he can watch herons, stilts, and oystercatchers fossick along the mud-flats and amongst the exposed sea-grass. Black swans in their thousands paddle in the shallow waters of the bay and feed on submerged sea grass. As dusk approaches large flights of terns, oystercatchers, gulls and swans wing their way across the bay, heading for their night-time roosting places. Amongst the trees on his land Mike can see and hear land-birds such as tui, fantail, quail, goldfinch, wood pigeon, silvereye, and his favourite: the bellbird. The tuis and bellbirds compete to be the best songsters. They dominate the dawn chorus and the bird-song at dusk. The call of the bellbird reminds Mike that he owns a special place. European colonisation of New Zealand presaged massive destruction of bird habitats, as farmers cleared the forests and bush to make pastures for sheep and cattle. As the native habitat disappeared, so did much of the birdlife that depended on it. But Mike's land was eventually allowed to regenerate and the trees and birds have returned.

Each year, in late October, or early November, godwits start to arrive on the spit, having flown, non-stop, all the way from Alaska, or Siberia. They stay until March and then make the long return journey. Mike is in awe of these tremendous fliers. Their annual migration is an amazing feat of navigation and endurance and it is a real privilege for him to see them probing the mudflats along the spit for worms and crabs.

* * * * *

Staying at the caravan in Puponga during holiday times and long weekends had always been very therapeutic for Mike. He could leave behind the pressures of work, and chores at home, and enjoy quality time with his family. In such a peaceful and tranquil place he could relax and re-charge. Now, he intended to re-start his life and make a permanent home for himself here. He hoped this would allow him to heal and face the future. He intended to build something that would be uniquely his own and he would do his utmost to avoid any negative impact on his environment. He wanted the birds to stay and he liked the idea of creating an eco-sustainable house.

Mike's qualifications and experience as a civil engineer meant that he was able to design the type of home he envisaged. He was fit enough and had sufficient skills to be able to do most of the structural work himself. He would have to engage a plumber, a glazier, and an electrician though. What appealed to him most about building at Puponga was the chance to throw himself whole-heartedly into a project that could consume all his waking hours and take his mind off the loneliness and despair of life without Rosie, his partner for thirty-seven years. And when he got too tired from the physical work involved he could give himself a break, take out his water-colours, and paint some of the local landscapes and wild-life. There was plenty of subject matter in and around Puponga to keep him going for years if he wanted.

Painting landscapes and wild-life was something Mike had decided to try before he faced retirement. Knowing he would need a significant interest to pursue when he gave up his career, he had been to night classes to learn the basics and, to his surprise, had found that he had quite a talent. He was certainly good enough to produce saleable art and had allowed some local galleries to display his work and sell on commission. So he had decided he would make water-colour painting his main activity in retirement. The design for his new home would certainly incorporate a studio and gallery.

CHAPTER 2.

It took Mike nearly six weeks to prepare plans and specifications for his new house and then he had to wait almost two months to be granted his building permit. He used this time to organise the supply of the building materials he would need and to obtain quotes for the plumbing, electrical and glazing work. So, as soon as he received his permit, he was ready to start. After three months of living in the confined space of his caravan he had plenty of motivation to begin building.

Mike had chosen to build his house directly in front of the escarpment. There was no way he was going to clear fell a large area and bulldoze a building platform. He wanted to preserve the natural contours of the land and leave the mature trees undisturbed. He did not intend to make a design statement with his house. It would not stand out for all to see, because he wanted it to merge into its surroundings as much as possible. It would be framed by the trees that had grown on his land for a lifetime. He intended to collect all the rain water from a clay tile roof and pipe it to a large storage tank. A pump would then supply the water to the kitchen, toilet, bathroom and laundry. All the rooms of the house were to be on one elevated tiled floor, with a large basement area underneath, where he could park his car and his boat, install a bank of batteries, and construct a small utility room and workshop. He intended to use a combination of solar and wind power for heating, cooking, lighting and the water pump. He planned to lay an array of solar panels along his roof and also erect a wind turbine back up on the hill. These would keep the batteries charged and provide sufficient electricity for his needs. The elevation of the living area, comprising an open-plan kitchen-dining-lounge space, two en suited bedrooms and a studio-gallery, ensured panoramic views out across the entire Puponga inlet. A large wooden deck was to be built at this level and run the full length of the building. Every room would open onto the deck, allowing maximum indoor-outdoor living. The external walls of the house were to be built of inter-locking pine logs and the voids below the tiled floor and above the ceilings would be heavily insulated using sheep's wool. The openings from the rooms to the deck were to be fitted with full-height, double-glazed wood-framed panels that could be completely or partially opened, or be kept closed, depending on the weather conditions. Finally, a natural composting system would be installed to deal with sewage and waste water from the kitchen and bathrooms. The resultant fertiliser and treated water was going to provide ideal nutrients for the garden Mike was going to create.

*****

On the first day of building Mike took stock of himself as he prepared his breakfast. Here he was, a sixty-three-year-old retiree about to start building his own house; well most of it . . . He was reasonably healthy, but was he fit enough to handle the physical demands of the job? Time would tell . . . He was determined, but he thought he might have to take care to pace himself whilst he built up his strength. He was a well proportioned six-footer, but he had to admit his muscles could do with some building up.

When he looked at himself in the mirror he thought he saw a reasonably young looking man for his age, not unattractive. He had clear blue eyes and a full head of hair, now mostly grey. Currently, though, he was looking a bit scruffy. He hadn't shaved for some days and he was overdue for a haircut. He shrugged and thought, 'I'm not trying to impress anyone. There's no-one here *to* impress!'

In the last few weeks Mike had become aware how little opportunity there was in Puponga for human contact. Each day, around lunch-time, he would take a thirty minute walk along the beach and part of the estuary, or if the tide was low he'd walk out across the exposed mud-flats to see how many seals were resting on the island and then continued on around the point of the peninsular. He seldom saw another person, but he often saw signs that some of the houses had occupants; perhaps some smoke rising from a chimney, or the sound of someone cutting firewood with an axe or chainsaw, or a small boat heading out along the channel, bound for a favoured fishing spot. So he found himself looking forward to seeing people on his thirty-centimetre television set each evening and catching up with whatever was happening in the world.

With breakfast over, Mike threw his dishes into the sink. He would deal with them later. Right now he wanted to try out the digger he had hired to cut trenches for the concrete foundations. He stepped out of the caravan with an air of excitement and strode over to the digger. He could hear a tui calling and he paused to watch a pair of fantails fluttering around a manuka tree, trying to flush out insects. They were such wonderful fliers, using their unique tail feathers to quickly duck and dive, and change direction as they chased and caught the insects as they flew. He settled into the cab of the digger and hoped the tuis and bellbirds would not be too distressed by the noise he was about to make, but he was sure that thrushes and blackbirds would stick around. As he dug he would be exposing a lot of worms and grubs. They would have a feast!

Mike wondered what Paul, or Julia would think if they could see him now, driving the digger to the site of his first cut. He hoped they would be impressed. In reality, though, they would be totally oblivious and fully focussed on their high-paced lives in London, where they had chosen to advance their careers: Julia as an interior designer and Paul as a book publisher. It had been great to see them again when they came home for their mother's funeral. However, afterwards, the three of them had been weighed down by their sadness and thoughts of their previous life as a family, and the time they could spend with him was all too short. They had to get back to their families and jobs in London, and there hadn't been much talk of what the future would bring.

'I must continue to make the effort to keep in regular contact with them,' Mike murmured to himself.

Chapter 3.

April 2008

During the last few days Mike had noticed activity in the old cabin on the adjacent plot of land. He hadn't seen anyone use the cabin for years and didn't know who owned it, but it seemed someone was living there now. It wasn't a usual time for holiday makers to be in the area, but someone had moved in. He had heard the noise of a car driving up the gravel path to the cabin and the chopping of firewood. Today, he noticed some washing on a makeshift clothesline.

As he walked across the road to the beach, at the start of his midday walk, Mike saw a woman walking towards the cabin. He wasn't close enough to tell her age, but noticed she had long black hair and was wearing a brown wind-jacket and blue jeans. There didn't seem to be anyone else around.

Having someone living close at hand was a new experience. For nearly three months Mike had been working hard every day and the few people he had seen were mostly truck-drivers delivering building materials. He had waved to some of the locals, but it seemed they were always at a distance and happy to remain that way. Perhaps that would apply to his new neighbour too?

As the tide was out Mike decided to walk out to the island, ford the channel and walk around the peninsular. He counted a dozen seals lying amongst the rocks and made sure he didn't disturb them. As he looked out to sea he saw a great many black swans bobbing amongst wavelets. Closer at hand a group of oystercatchers were strutting along the channel, stopping occasionally to prod their beaks into the mud and generally looking very important and busy.

A half-hour later Mike was back and, as he approached his gate, he looked across at the next-door cabin. It was set well back from the road and was partially obscured by kanuka trees and tree ferns, but he thought he saw movement behind a window. Then the front door opened and the women he had seen earlier stepped out. She stopped short as she saw him and stood looking at him for a moment. Hesitantly, she gave a cursory wave before turning away and disappearing round behind the cabin. Mike returned the wave, but he didn't know if his response had been seen.

'She looks to be about forty . . . and she has a rather graceful, dignified manner about her,' he thought. 'Good heavens! I'm getting far too curious about this woman . . . Get a grip, Robinson!'

He was still thinking about his neighbour and wondering what had brought her to Puponga when he resumed his work with the roof trusses.

For the last eleven weeks Mike had worked twelve hours a day on his house and had made significant progress. He had completed the concrete footings for his foundations and the concrete floor of the basement quite quickly. A timber mill in Richmond had cut his logs so they would interlock when placed one on another and had delivered them to the site. Mike had then spent some weeks building the walls that would form the basement of his house and support everything above. He had been able to use the digger he had hired to lift each log and lower it so that it slotted into place. Laying the joists for the floor of his main living space and the adjoining deck was next and, in the last few days, he had finished assembling the exterior walls of his living areas.

He had needed to hire a large crane to lift and position the interlocking logs above the basement structure. Using hand signals to guide the crane driver, he soon established a routine. The whole job was finished in just two days. Then, before the crane was returned, he arranged for prefabricated roof trusses to be winched up and lowered into position, one by one. Mike had to fix them in place and cross-brace them, so that they were rigid and secure. It was hard work for one man, but he was resourceful and he had become stronger.

Mike was proud of his progress and was delighted the size and shape of his house was starting to be revealed, despite the surrounding scaffolding. There were no windows, doors, or floors yet, but they would be installed once the roof had been sarked and tiled. That was his main priority now, with winter approaching. He wanted to have roof cover before the weather deteriorated and made it impractical and unpleasant to work without shelter.

* * * * *

The next day Mike decided to vary his midday routine and head up to the Farewell Spit lookout. He took a tree-lined track that ran inland a bit, but parallel with the beach road. The track took him to a gravel road that crossed a bridge at the main outlet of the estuary and then climbed up the hill to a car park. From there it was just a two-hundred metre climb to reach the lookout, one hundred and fifty metres above sea level. The views from the lookout were spectacular. Mike could see the spit curving off into the distance and disappearing at the horizon. On a clear day he knew he would be able to glimpse a stand of old pine trees at the very end of the spit, where there was a lighthouse that used to be manned before automation came along. Today, though, the wind was blowing quite hard and there was too much moisture in the air. He could see sheets of salt spray lashing the lower dunes near the beach and clouds of sand swirling up from the higher dunes along the central spine of the spit. He turned around to look back down to his piece of land and could just make out some of the roof trusses. He was pleased that his house would be mostly obscured by the surrounding kanuka and karaka trees. Out in the bay he spied a commercial fishing boat dredging for scallops. He looked for black swans, but the wind was creating a rough sea near the shoreline and he thought the swans were likely to be sheltering inland, probably annoying the hell out of some farmer by helping themselves to his pasture and pooping everywhere!

Turning a corner of the wooded track on his return journey Mike nearly bumped into his next-door neighbour. He had been head down, deep in thought. Startled, he stepped to one side and smiled apologetically at the woman who had loomed before him. As they paused to look at each other Mike felt an immediate spark of something. The woman had returned his gaze and, just for a second or two, it was as though everything had gone quiet and stopped. The moment was fleeting, though, and the woman gave a wry smile as she nodded to him and then continued on her way without speaking. Mike remained standing there and turned to watch her walk off.

'What happened then?' he wondered. He felt as if some kind of connection had just taken place. It had felt as though a small charge of energy had travelled through him. This had never happened before. It was a bit disturbing and he wondered about it. Certainly the lady had surprised him . . . and not just because she suddenly appeared out of nowhere. He had looked up to see a very striking and attractive Maori. She had immediately reminded him of a young Kiri Te Kanawa, but in blue jeans rather than the full-length gown that Kiri always wore for her operatic performances. The likeness was uncanny and this woman seemed to have the same poise as the singer. She had looked at him intently when they had met on the track and he wondered if she had felt the same charge of energy he had. It was weird . . . and it left him feeling at little foolish.

'Get a grip, Robinson,' he muttered to himself. 'You are a sixty-three-year-old widower for God's sake. She must be twenty years younger!'

But as he walked off he knew he wanted to meet this lady.

'Can't hurt to be neighbourly can it?' he muttered.

But then he murmured, 'Who are you kidding, Robinson? Living like a hermit these last few months must be getting to me . . . *and* I'm starting to talk to myself!'

Chapter 4.

The next day Mike was finishing a lunch of cheese and tomato sandwiches as he listened to the end of the midday news hour on his radio. Hearing a car drive up to his caravan he realised he must have left his front gate open. On opening the door he was surprised to see his next-door neighbour step from a silver Honda CRV. She had obviously been off-road somewhere as her boots and jeans were spattered with mud. As she approached Mike was again struck by the graceful way she held herself and moved, and he realised she possessed some kind of charisma that was intriguing him.

'Hello,' Mike said as he smiled and stepped down to meet her.

'Kia ora. I hope you don't mind me driving in . . .'

She paused as she noticed the half-finished sandwich in Mike's hand and said, 'Oh. I'm sorry to interrupt your lunch. I didn't realise it was that time already. Look, I was going to ask if you could spare half an hour to help me, but maybe . . .'

Mike interrupted.

'I've no problem with you driving in . . . and I was just finishing my lunch. What kind of help do you need?'

'Well, if you're sure . . . I've been walking across the farm to Fossil Point and I've found a sheep that's got itself stuck in a creek. I think it's been there for ages, because it looks pretty distressed. I wasn't able to pull it out by myself, it's far too heavy for me, sunken down into the mud like it is, and I can't find anyone at the farmhouse to help. I think they must be away for a day or two, because there is no vehicle in the garage. I was thinking that the two of us, together, might be able to get the poor thing out.'

'OK. I'll be happy to try. I usually go out for a walk about now anyway. Let me just get my boots on and I'll look for some rope. We might need something to pull on if we can't get a good grip on the animal . . . and a shovel might be a good idea too. My name's Mike by the way . . .'

'Thank you, Mike. I'm so pleased you were at home, because I don't think it will survive much longer. Goodness knows how long it's been trapped . . . I'm Mereana, and you probably know I've been next door for the last few days.'

Mike sat on the step to his caravan door to pull on his boots and said, 'Well I'm happy to meet you Mereana, and it's nice to think there's someone else around. I have seen you a couple of times from a distance . . . and of course I nearly bowled you over yesterday didn't I!

'Well, I think we were both a bit surprised to find someone else on the track . . . and you did look as though you were rather pre-occupied.'

'I was a bit . . . trying to work out a tricky problem with my roof.'

'I've heard you banging and sawing and drilling. Sounds like a hive of industry over here and, now that I can see what it is you've been working on, I have to say I'm impressed. Have you been doing all that by yourself?'

'For the most part . . . and I'm really enjoying playing Bob the Builder.'

'Is the place going to be for your own use? The views from up there must be fantastic.'

'That's right . . . It's my first big retirement project.'

'Well, good for you . . . um . . . Mike.'

'One way of keeping out of trouble I suppose . . . Shall we head off to have a look at your sheep?'

Mereana opened the door of the CRV for him and then walked round to take her seat behind the wheel. Mike placed a coil of rope and a shovel behind the back seat and slid into the passenger seat.

As Mereana backed up and then started out towards the gate she said, 'It will just take us five minutes to drive to the end of the track and then we have to walk for about another five or ten minutes to the creek where the sheep is. We'll have to climb down from the track and it's pretty muddy there.'

'I'm not going to be bothered by a bit of mud. Let's just hope we can get the poor thing out. Being stuck in a bog and starving to death must be a horrible way to die . . .'

'I'm so glad I spotted it, because there don't seem to be many people about. It would be easy to walk past without even knowing it was there and in trouble.'

'Got to be this sheep's lucky day then,' Mike said with a smile. 'Is that your place next door? I haven't seen you there before, or anyone else come to that . . .'

'No. It belongs to an old school-friend. She doesn't know what to do with the place, because she lives up north now. She's just happy to let me use it for a while.'

'Are you there on your own?'

'Yes. It's just me . . . I'm enjoying a bit of time-out.'

'Planning on staying on for a bit then?'

'For the time being anyway . . . I've no plans really . . .'

Mike thought her last comment sounded a bit forlorn, but he decided not to ask anything more.

'Well, while you're there, if there's anything you need, I'm just fifty metres away . . . Don't hesitate.'

'That's really good of you, Mike. I'll bear that in mind. Looks like you are also on your own. Are you taking time-out too?'

Mike thought about the way she had referred to time-out . . . twice now.

'Yes to being on my own, but it's not really time-out, more like a new beginning. I lost my wife six months ago and I decided to come here to start over. I'm retired now, so I can enjoy living here, away from what I was used to . . . and I enjoy the peace and beauty of the place.'

Mike was conscious of Mereana's reaction when he spoke about losing Rosie. She had turned slightly to quickly glance at him. He wondered how he had come to open up to her so quickly. He also wondered what had caused Mereana to need some time-out.

'I'm sorry to hear about your wife. It must be . . .'

Mike quickly interrupted.

'Thanks, but I try to look to the future now . . .'

Mereana read the signal loud and clear. This wasn't something he wanted to talk about and nothing more was said until they reached the parking area at the start of the track.

After Mike retrieved the rope and shovel from the back of the CRV Mereana led the way along the narrow track and, for the most part, they walked in silence, each occupied with their own thoughts.

After a few minutes Mike said, 'The weather is being kind to us at least. It doesn't look as though there's any rain on the way.'

'The wind has a bite to it though,' Mereana replied. 'It must be coming from way down south somewhere.'

Mereana suddenly stopped walking and Mike accidently bumped into her.

'Oops. Sorry,' he said.

Mereana chuckled.

'My fault I think . . . Look. There it is . . . Can you see? Down there just past that cabbage tree.'

'Where? Oh yes. Gosh, you must have sharp eyesight to have spotted it. It's not that easy to see, even when you're looking for it . . . Let's get down and see what can be done.'

Mike could see the creature was in a bad way, but it still bleated weakly as they approached. Trying to lift it out proved impossible for Mike on his own, so the two of them went to each side of the animal and tried to pull together. That didn't work either. The sheep was quite large, was well down into the mud, and its wool was saturated with creek water.

'OK,' Mike said. 'It looks like we'll have to dig a trench, so we can pull the old girl into it and then up the bank.'

It didn't take Mike long to get a rope around the helpless animal and Mereana started to dig a channel in front of it. As Mike took over and starting to dig in earnest Mereana stood back and watched. She noted the ease with which Mike worked and realised she had been enjoying his company. She had quickly felt at ease with him, something that was quite surprising to her given the troubles she had experienced in recent months.

When the trench was finished they both took hold of the rope and started to pull, gently at first and then with more power. The sheep bleated some more, but didn't budge.

'Let's try me pushing it from the back end, whilst you continue to pull on the rope,' Mike suggested.

They took up their positions again and heaved. This time the sheep slithered forward and fell to its knees. Recovering, it stood up and remained there panting. It was out of the mud, but was seemingly unable to climb the bank by itself.

'I'll come up onto the bank now and we'll have another go at pulling together. OK?'

'Yes. I think she's probably just exhausted and confused. If we can get her up here she'll probably be fine.'

'Let's do it then.'

When they started pulling the sheep towards the bank the animal finally realised that its legs were no longer trapped in mud and it was able to teeter up the slope. Mereana and Mike were breathing hard from the effort of pulling such a heavy weight.

'Goodness she's big,' Mereana gasped. 'I think she might be pregnant.'

'Could be . . . She's hefty all right . . . Can you just hold her whilst I untie the rope?'

With the rope off, they both stepped away. The sheep stood there panting, looked at them for a minute, and then slowly walked off towards a patch of grass. As it lowered its head to eat Mike said, 'Job done. That old girl owes you her life, Mereana!'

'She owes you too, Mike. I'm so pleased you could help.'

'Yes, well . . . it's a good feeling, seeing her safe like that . . .'

They walked back quickly. They were both soaking wet and covered in mud from their time in the creek, Mike more so as he had used his arms and shoulders to heave the ewe clear of the mud. The wind was quite chilling, especially when they crested the ridge before the descent to the car park.

In the car they warmed up quite quickly and, as they drove back to Puponga, Mereana asked about the kind of house Mike was building. He gave her an outline, but he could tell by the nature of her questions that she couldn't really visualise how it would look when finished.

'Why don't you come over sometime? I'll show you the drawings and give you a guided tour,' he said.

'I'd love to, Mike, if you're sure you don't mind . . .'

'Not at all! It will be a pleasure. You might get a bit bored though. I know what it can be like when people start blathering on about their hobby horses . . .'

'I'm sure I won't be bored. I am genuinely interested. I think it must be immensely satisfying to design and build your own house . . . and doing it all by yourself must be quite a challenge, especially if you aren't a builder by trade . . .'

'No, I'm not a builder, but I can design structures. I trained as a civil engineer.'

'Oh. Well that must help I guess.'

'Yes, but I won't be able to do everything myself. I'll have to hire people like electricians and plumbers to do things I don't have the skills to do . . . Look, do you mind dropping me off at your gate? I want to get out of these clothes and take a shower.'

'Sure. I'm going to do the same. I'm sorry to have disrupted your afternoon . . . The least I can do is offer you coffee . . . and I have some muffins. How about I provide afternoon tea in about an hour?'

'I'm glad you asked for my help, Mereana. It was good to save that old girl and I enjoyed your company. The coffee and muffins sound too good to refuse, so shall I pop over around three o'clock?'

'Perfect! I'll see you then.'

As Mike got out of the car he smiled at Mereana and felt another frisson of energy as he saw her smile in response. Her eyes seemed to see right into his being.

Heading off to the caravan and a warm shower Mike realised he was feeling excited at the prospect of afternoon tea with Mereana.

'Settle down you old fool,' he muttered. She's young enough to be your daughter and you know absolutely nothing about her.'

CHAPTER 5.

As Mike approached Mereana's cabin he suddenly became aware of raised voices coming from within. Then he noticed there were now two cars in the driveway. Obviously a visitor had arrived. Mike stopped and wondered if he should continue up to the door when there was a burst of angry shouting.

He heard Mereana call out, 'Leave me alone! Can't you understand? . . . I'm finished with you! I'm not coming back! It's over . . . I've had enough!'

Then he heard a man's voice snarl menacingly, 'Don't think you can walk out on me, you cow! You'll be coming back all right . . . I'll make sure of that!'

Mike was at the point of turning back when he heard Mereana scream, 'Don't you dare hit me!' and then the man's furious reply, 'I'm going to teach you what happens when you bring whakama to me and the whanau, you selfish bitch!'

The door burst open and Mereana came out running, a terrified look on her face. She saw Mike instantly, but ran straight past him and out towards the road. As he turned to watch her run he heard another shout.

'There's nowhere you can run to! I'll always find you!'

Feeling shocked and confused Mike turned back to see a middle-aged Maori man charge out of the cabin, obviously intent on pursuing Mereana. Seeing Mike standing there he stopped short and scowled angrily.

'Who are you? What are you doing here?' he demanded.

Mike was astonished at how aggressive the man looked and by the rude tone of his questioning. He decided to try to keep calm and see if he could do something to defuse what was obviously some kind of domestic dispute.

'I'm a neighbour. My name's Mike. It would be good to know who you are and what on earth is going on here. Mereana is obviously frightened of you.'

Mike held his ground and waited for a response. Clearly the man was trying to decide what to do.

'This has nothing to do with you,' he said forcibly. 'Stay out of it! This is between me and my wife . . . and she has some explaining to do!'

'Well, I don't think you are going to get anywhere by your threatening behaviour. I just heard enough to know that the two or you are not going to be sitting down for a cosy chat any time soon.'

'As I said, it's not your business. I want you out of here, now!'

'I'm happy to leave, but I suggest you leave too. If there is something you want from Mereana right now is obviously not a good time to get it. You are clearly very angry about something, but threats and violence won't get you whatever it is you want. She just ran past me looking terrified! I'd suggest you go away, calm down, and try another more rational approach some other time.'

Mereana's husband stood looking at Mike. He was extremely tense, blinking hard, his mouth working, clenching and unclenching his fists. Mike was starting to think the man was about to take a swing at him when he suddenly relaxed and shook his head.

'That's probably good advice,' he said grudgingly. 'But you have nothing to do with this and I don't want you involved. Stay out of it!'

With that the man turned and trudged towards the second car in the driveway. He got in, started up, drove past Mike without a glance, turned onto the road and sped away. Mike realised he had been holding his breath and let it out in a long sigh. He had come very close to getting into a fight and he felt very relieved that it hadn't come to that. He thought he might have come off second best.

Mike found Mereana sitting on the step to his caravan. She had obviously been crying and was looking very anxious and ashamed.

'I'm so sorry, Mike. I didn't expect anything like this, but he is so proud and losing his mana is making him act crazy. I guess you must have convinced him to go away . . . I saw his car drive by . . .'

'I did suggest he leave, but I think he'll be back again to try to achieve whatever he came for.'

'I'm so embarrassed . . . and I'm ashamed! I just ran and left you there to face him . . . I um . . . wasn't in a very good state and I was truly frightened he was going to hit me . . . I'm so sorry, Mike . . .'

'Don't feel bad on my account, Mereana. I'm just happy I was able to defuse things a bit, for now anyway . . . Look, come inside and I'll make us that coffee we were going to have. It might help if you tell me what's going on, but if you'd rather not we'll have the coffee anyway. Totally up to you . . .'

'OK, Mike. Coffee would be good and I don't feel like going back to the cabin just yet. If you can bear it, I'd like to stay . . . just for a bit . . . and I'll try to explain what has happened between Tamati and me.'

'Well, only if you want to . . . Sometimes it can help to talk about a problem . . . you know . . . to put it into perspective . . . But this is clearly family business and I'm not exactly a counsellor. We've only just met and we know nothing about each other. '

'I know, but I would like to tell you, Mike. I don't want you wondering if I've been unfaithful to my husband, or anything like that . . .'

Mike quickly interrupted.

'That thought really hasn't crossed my mind at all! I have no idea, but I guess something serious has to have happened. You have obviously left your husband and he is evidently very unhappy about it . . . He was probably right to tell me it's none of my business.'

'Yes, but if you can bear it I'd like talk.'

'All right . . . Let's make the coffee first. Come in and sit yourself down . . . if you can find your way through my mess . . .'

* * * * *

That night Mike lay in his bed thinking about what Mereana had told him. She had talked for more than an hour and he had hardly spoken a word. It was as though she had bottled everything up and suddenly needed to release it all.

She had explained how she and Tamati had both grown up in Nelson. Their respective families were very active in all things Maori and they spent a great deal of time at Waimea Marae. Mereana and Tamati had been identified from an early age as having leadership qualities. As they grew up they were encouraged to become highly proficient in using the Maori language. The kaumatuas at the marae had carefully guided them in all aspects of Maori culture and they always had leading roles in kapa haka. They knew that they had been selected and then groomed as leaders and role models for younger Maori. During their high school years and beyond they were constantly engaged in the same events and programmes, spending huge amounts of time at the marae organising and taking part in nearly all the activities. It was inevitable that they became drawn to each other. When they both went to Christchurch for their tertiary education, Mereana studying to become a secondary school teacher and Tamati studying for a Bachelor of Commerce degree, they had time apart, but they were back together at the marae whenever they returned during term breaks and at Christmas. Following their graduation Mereana got a teaching job at Nayland College and Tamati was offered a job by Waimea Corporation, a company that managed a variety of Maori enterprises in horticulture, fishing and property development. So they were back in Nelson and were now being actively encouraged to make a future together. They were the epitome of what was best in young Maori leadership and everyone knew that, together, they were destined to make a huge contribution on behalf of their people in northern South Island.

Mike recalled how Mereana had said, 'Our kaumatuas would encourage me to marry Tamati. They said it would be the ideal marriage, because we were made for each other and had so much in common. At that age I was prepared to listen to them and accept their advice. I think I was excited and rather flattered by the way I had been favoured and nurtured and taught by them. To me they were very wise and deserved to be taken seriously. My parents also hoped I would eventually marry Tamati, so they supported the advice I was getting from our kaumatuas.'

Mereana and Tamati had been happy to fall into a relationship. They were both physically attractive and they enjoyed each other's company. As time went on they became aware that everyone was waiting for them to become engaged and then marry. It was just a matter of time. Neither of them really questioned this. In the past their relationship had been similar to that of a brother and sister and it wasn't difficult to see this continue. Mereana never believed she was in love with Tamati. She respected him, and there were times when they had great fun together, but what she felt for him always fell short of what she imagined love to be. However, she could feel the heavy weight of expectation from her parents and everyone at the marae that she and Tamati should marry. She knew Tamati felt much the way she did. They were both quite prepared to enjoy sex with each other; they certainly had the same desire as anyone else to achieve that kind of pleasure, but whilst that seemed to be enough for Tamati, it was never quite enough for Mereana.

Eventually, after they had been married for two years, Mereana decided to confront Tamati and tell him she wanted them to have some time apart. She wanted to live separately for a while whilst she decided if she wanted to remain married to him. But just when she had plucked up enough courage to approach Tamati about this she discovered she was pregnant. So she resolved to carry on as before and Tamati never learned that she was so disillusioned with their marriage. When her son, Matiu, was born she threw herself into motherhood and tried to forget about her discontent. Then, eighteen months later, she gave birth to a lovely daughter, Huia, and so she continued as before, but always wondering if she would ever know true fulfilment.

In his last year at high school Matiu won an athletic scholarship offered by the University of Hawaii. He left Nelson the following year to spend the next three to four years in Honolulu gaining a degree and representing the University in middle-distance track events. At the same time Huia was granted a student exchange scholarship to spend her final high school year in Copenhagen, Denmark. Suddenly, with her children overseas, Mereana had time and opportunity to consider her future. By this time Tamati had become the main spokesman and negotiator for Maori living in the Nelson-Golden Bay region. He was always busy with research and meetings, and often travelled away as he gathered information about the injustices local Maori tribes had suffered in the period of colonisation of New Zealand. He had been given the task of preparing a claim to the Waitangi Tribunal that would seek redress and compensation for the wrongs Maori had suffered during the period of British administration of New Zealand, after the signing of the Treaty of Waitangi in 1840. The Treaty was supposed to protect the interests of the indigenous Maori, but in reality there were numerous occasions when their lands were usurped. It wasn't until 1975 that a more enlightened administration decided to redress past wrongs and establish the Waitangi Tribunal to hear all claims and recommend how grievances could be resolved.

Preparing a claim for redress, after all these years, was a major undertaking and a huge responsibility. Tamati was totally consumed by the work involved. He had to be able to verify the facts of every injustice and he had to determine what land, or other resource could reasonably be claimed from the Government now, many years after land-grabs and other events had occurred. He tried to think like a lawyer, because the claim he would present on behalf of his people would be considered in a forum not unlike a traditional court of law. Only a well-researched and compelling claim would be rewarded with the kind of redress that would allow his people to accept that their grievances could be put aside and they could move on. Tamati hoped that the land and other resources he would claim in compensation would form the basis for new business ventures, providing more work and a better standard of living for Maori living in the region.

The claim was being referred to as the Wakatu-Mohua Claim; Wakatu being the name of an early Maori settlement in what is now Nelson and Mohua being the Maori name for Golden Bay. The claim was going to be a composite claim for the entire Nelson-Golden Bay region. Throughout the many months it took Tamati to research and gather evidence for the claim, and to consult with representatives of each of the iwi claimants, he saw little of Mereana. He would often arrive home late and exhausted and quickly go to bed. In the mornings he would leave early and he relied totally on Mereana to look after their children, their household, and their responsibilities at the marae. This was quite a burden, on top of her teaching responsibilities at Nayland College, but Mereana knew that Tamiti was doing vitally important work and that he was under severe time pressure to have the claim ready before the Government's imposed deadline. She accepted that he only came home to sleep. In fact, she found she didn't resent his absence. That was when she realised she no longer had any need to maintain their previous relationship. Her children were now young adults and would soon be making their own way in the world. She could now confront her unhappiness and wish to try something else.

When Mereana first spoke to Tamati about her desire for a separation he became extremely defensive and did not want to hear, or talk about her need to explore alternatives to the life they had been living. He expressed his anger and disbelief that she could think of such a thing. What about their position in the Maori community? What would their children think? How could she even think of leaving him and cause him to massively lose mana? No, he didn't want to change anything and he was not prepared to try to understand why Mereana was unhappy. She would have to toughen up and live the life that had been pre-ordained for her.

'You are not just married to me . . . you are married to this way of life. It is your duty, just as it is mine. I'll hear no more of this!' he had said emphatically.

A few months later nothing had changed and Mereana again told Tamati that she needed to leave. This time Tamati became so angry that he vented his frustration by hitting Mereana several times and hard enough to knock her to the floor.

Mereana had explained, 'When I insisted that I needed time-out he just lost it. He was so furious! I think he hit me because I was in danger of upsetting his high standing in our community. He thinks of himself as a rangatira and he could not bear the loss of face he thought would occur if people believed he didn't have what it took to hold on to his wife. I'm quite sure he wouldn't have lost any of *his* mana. It would be *me* that would be seen as disloyal and to be abandoning everything I was supposed to be doing for my people . . . not that I ever would abandon them. I suddenly saw something in Tamati I had never seen before. He became very aggressive and really thought he could physically intimidate me and force me to stay with him. I tried talking to him again, about three weeks later, and again he hit me and told me he wouldn't hear any talk of separation, even temporarily. I was really struggling to deal with the fact that my husband thought he could beat me to achieve what he wanted. I was really unhappy and felt I couldn't let things go on like this. So, about a week later I tried to talk to Tamati again. *Still* he wouldn't accept anything I was saying and this time he really laid into me. It was the last straw. I knew then that I *had* to leave. When I telephoned my best friend, Annabelle, to tell her what I was planning, she told me about Puponga and how I could use the cabin here. I moved out the next day and didn't tell Tamati, or anyone else, where I was going. I still have to ring Matiu and Huia to tell them what I've done . . . and I also need to go and see my parents. If they've heard from Tamati they'll be getting upset I haven't spoken to them yet . . . I just haven't had the courage to do it all, so far, but I can't wait much longer.

'Since I have been here, even though it has only been a few days, I have felt such a sense of relief. I have started to relax and I have felt good . . . even excited about planning a new life of my own . . . I already know, for certain, that I was right to leave Tamati. I definitely won't go back to him . . . And I've been surprised at how much I love it here, even though it's such a small and isolated place. I have a sense that I have been called to this place. Perhaps it is because some of my ancestors used to live here. I went to the old pa site on the peninsular yesterday and I experienced some very strange feelings there. It was as though my forebears were acknowledging me somehow. I know this sounds a bit spooky, and a bit irrational, but it was how I felt . . . and I was glad. Anyway, for now at least, Puponga seems to be the perfect place for me to do my writing . . . I've written small pieces before, but have never had much time for it. I've always wanted to write a novel . . .'

Mereana had given Mike a lot to think over and a number of questions flashed through his mind. He hadn't had a chance to ask anything, though, as she had suddenly stood up and moved to the door of the caravan.

'Thanks for listening, Mike,' she had said. 'I've probably said more than I should . . . I'll go now and try to get myself together . . . See you . . .'

And with that she had stepped outside. Mike was left to wonder what had caused her to leave so unexpectedly. He had been caught by surprise and was left sitting there, staring at the door Mereana had closed behind her.

CHAPTER 6.

The weather had turned for the worse during the night. Mike woke briefly and heard the wind whistling through the kanuka and toi toi that sheltered his caravan. In the morning when he looked out dark clouds were looming from the south and he felt moisture in the air. It would be raining in two to three hours, he thought.

Wanting to make best use of the time he had before the rain Mike had a quick breakfast and then headed outside to start hoisting sarking planks onto his roof. He calculated that he could perhaps get about thirty planks up and nailed down before he would have to call it a day.

He had rigged up a pulley system, but still found hauling the timber up to the roof physically demanding. Nailing the planks to the roof trusses was easier, but hard on his knees and he was thankful for his knee protectors. It took him until just past midday to finish nailing down the thirty boards. He descended to ground level and looked up to survey his handiwork. About a quarter of the roof was now covered.

Turning towards his caravan he felt the first heavy spots of rain being driven before the approaching front.

'The weather's about to pack up,' he thought. 'Maybe I'll get some painting done this afternoon.'

It had been weeks since Mike had pulled out his easel and water-colours. He had a part-finished painting of a group of oystercatchers fossicking along the shoreline that he wanted to return to.

He was about to heat up some stew leftover from the night before and make a cup of tea when he heard Mereana call his name. Looking out, he saw her approaching with a covered tray.

'Kia ora, Mike! I hope you don't mind, but I've brought some lunch for you . . . I've heard you hammering for hours and I thought you might like to have a break from fixing lunch for yourself.'

'That's very kind of you! How can I possibly say no . . . ? You didn't have to bother, though, I'm quite used to making my own meals. Better come on in . . . it's starting to rain and it's going to bucket down in a few minutes.'

'Thanks, Mike. It's no bother at all and I must admit I've brought enough for both of us. I wanted to do something to show my appreciation for you being such a hero and fantastic listener yesterday, so I've brought some quiche and a salad!'

'That would certainly beat my lunch-making efforts hands down . . . but look, Mereana, you shouldn't feel any need to try to repay me . . . I only did what any right-minded person would do in the circumstances.'

'Perhaps . . . but I really do feel grateful . . . I hope you don't mind, but I do like to have someone to cook for apart from myself. I have to cook anyway, so it's really no trouble . . .'

'As I said, you shouldn't feel any need to repay me . . . Returning a favour shouldn't be necessary amongst friends . . . and I hope we are going to be friends . . . ?'

'I hope so too, Mike, and I promise that, if I cook for you, there will be no strings attached. It won't be because I feel the need to return a favour . . . It will simply be that I get pleasure from cooking. There . . . can we settle on that?'

Mike laughed.

'OK, but I suspect you just found a way to get round my objections.'

'Mike, I can assure you that anyone who turns their nose up at my food is going to miss out on a treat. I am known for my culinary prowess and I like to keep demonstrating it. I'm not averse to a few compliments on what I serve up either . . .'

'All right . . . I give in! I will submit to your culinary talents.'

* * * * *

The quiche was really delicious and Mike was impressed.

'Wow! That was great! I don't believe I've ever had a quiche as good as that and you did something to the salad that made it really tangy.'

'Don't you go trying to discover my secret recipes, because my lips are sealed!'

'All right. There's no way I can endure water torture, so your secrets are safe from me!'

Mereana smiled attractively and then her expression changed to a troubled look.

'About yesterday, Mike, you really were a great help and you probably saved me from getting bashed and dragged out of here kicking and screaming. I've never seen Tamati so furious . . . and it helped tremendously to talk to you about things. I'm not sure why I felt I could unload all that onto a person I've only just met, but it helped so much to talk . . . and you were so patient. I did burble on quite a bit and, when I suddenly realised how much I had said, I thought I'd better stop and not drag you into my problems . . .'

'You paid me the compliment of telling me your story and a lot of it *was* very personal. I'll keep what you said in confidence of course. What you explained raised a few questions, though, and I'd like to think I'll understand more if you are willing to talk again some time.'

'I'd love that, if you think you could stand it, but I don't know anything about you, Mike . . . Just that you lost your wife and you are trying to make a new start here.'

'What do you want to know?'

'Whatever you feel happy about telling me I guess . . .'

'OK . . . The weather's set in now, so no time like the present I think. I can't do any more outside today and it would be good to have your company. Let's see . . . I was born in Cambridge in England, but my parents decided to emigrate to New Zealand for a better life. That was just after the war, when I was just a youngster, and things were pretty tough then. I have some fleeting memories of life as a young boy in England and about the boat trip to New Zealand, but I don't really remember too much about where I came from. I've been back of course, but much has changed in the area where we lived. I don't feel any affinity with the place really. I have considered New Zealand my true home since I was in primary school and I am proud to have New Zealand citizenship.'

'Goodness! You don't have any English accent at all!'

'No. I became well and truly immersed in all things Kiwi I guess. All my friends are Kiwis. I played rugby, had all my schooling and went to university here, and have always worked for Kiwi businesses . . . except when I went to Europe in my twenties for the good old 'overseas experience'. And of course I married a Kiwi, a Christchurch girl . . . We had the best possible marriage and two lovely children. They were born and grew up in Nelson, but live in England now . . . and they both love it there. It's quite ironic really . . . They prefer my country of birth and I far prefer theirs! They were able to stay in the UK because they qualified for British Passports, on account of me being born over there. Now it seems that, unlike my parents, they see good opportunities for themselves and their families in England. I'm always hopeful they'll return one day, but Paul has an excellent job with a major book publisher and Julia is gaining a solid reputation as an interior designer. They both have English partners and children too. But maybe . . . when they come to realise they'll never be able to match our quality of life if they continue to live over there, they'll eventually see the light and come home . . . In the meantime there is a lot they like about the pace of life there, and being able to travel throughout Europe so easily is a major attraction for them.

'When they went it was really hard for Rosie. That's my wife. She missed them both terribly. I did too of course . . . and that hasn't changed. I try to make sure I don't leave it too long between emails and telephone calls, so we stay in touch. As you know, Rosie died . . . She was killed in a car crash about five months ago. Some German tourists had drifted onto the wrong side of the road whilst driving their campervan. They had been driving for a long time and were tired. They just forgot for a few moments that we drive on the left here. It happened on the highway south of Nelson. They went round a bend and smacked headlong into Rosie's car. She died instantly and the two Germans both ended up crippled for life . . . I don't hold a grudge any more, but I do think it has left me a bit . . . lost . . . in a way. Rosie was everything to me and I'll always miss her dearly. I had only just retired as a partner in a small civil engineering firm in Nelson and Rosie was thinking of giving up her job at Nelson Hospital . . . She was an occupational therapist. It's such a shame she was never able to do all the things she had planned. We both had a list of things we wanted to do. One thing she really wanted to try was pottery . . . and I wanted to develop my painting.'

'Losing Rosie like that must have been so awful for you, Mike. And I have been moaning about *my* troubles! You have been through so much more!'

'I think I have learned to deal with it now, Mereana . . . mostly anyway. I still feel a bit bereft from time to time, but I think I made the right decision to sell our house in Richmond and come here. There were far too many memories there and I do want to think positively about the next stage of my life. Deciding to build a house here has given me a project I can get my teeth into. The more I see everything taking shape, and realise that I am doing this myself . . . you know, my design, my labour and so on, the more I think I am doing something that will set me up for whatever turns up next. And Puponga is a very good place to find subjects for my landscape and wildlife paintings.'

Mike paused. He had been talking for a while now and he'd noticed how attentive Mereana had been. It felt good talking to her and she seemed genuinely interested. He was struck again by how she affected him. As she listened and watched him deal with his emotions it seemed that she connected with him somehow. He was beginning to feel she could become someone quite special to him . . . Perhaps he should be treading more carefully, he thought.

'I have just realised, Mereana . . . I don't know your last name. Mine's Robinson . . .'

'Mike Robinson . . . Hmm, that has a nice ring to it. My married name is Marshall . . . and I'll bet you were thinking it would be a Maori name. However, Tamati's great, great grandfather was a seaman who jumped ship to marry a Maori woman. My maiden name was Parata . . . Anyway, I think I've probably held you up long enough . . . I see you have your paints ready on the bench there. I'll get going and you can get on with your art. I'm planning to start some writing this afternoon, so we are both going to be in creative mode . . .'

With that Mereana collected the lunch things and placed them on her tray. Mike looked out of the window.

'You haven't held me up. I have all the time in the world. Anyway, it looks like the rain has eased. You shouldn't get too wet, but I have an old golf umbrella I can let you have.'

'I think I'll be fine, Mike. Thanks anyway. Good luck with your painting.'

As Mike got up to let Mereana out he said, 'Thanks for everything . . . and the lunch was a lovely surprise . . . What are you going to write about?'

'I'm not sure yet, but something will come to me . . . Bye!'

* * * * *

Mike put his part-finished painting of the oystercatchers on the easel and studied it for a moment. Then he shook his head and put the painting to one side. Reaching for a blank canvas he was already thinking about a new subject. It would be difficult to achieve the effect he was thinking of, but he thought, 'Why not . . . I'll give it a try.'

CHAPTER 7.

Once the sarking was finished the roofer was able to install the guttering and lay the roof tiles. Mike was lucky his timing suited the contractor. Jim Phillips had been able to start just as he was nailing down the last of the sarking planks. Completing the work was going to take three to four days, weather permitting.

When the roof and flooring were finished the windows and external doors could be fitted. These had been prefabricated and the glazier was waiting for word that he could proceed with their installation. The house would then be weather-tight and Mike would be able to set up a temporary studio for his painting. In the meantime the caravan made for a very cramped studio, even with the table folded away to make room for his easel and with his water-colours set out on the small kitchen bench. And Mike had to pack everything away at meal and bed times.

It was not often that Mike attempted a portrait painting and, until now, he had only done so with the subject sitting for him, or by referring to photographs. He didn't have either for his current subject. He didn't want Mereana to know he had decided to paint her, so he was relying on memory. He had decided on a head and shoulders portrait, with Mereana looking to her left along the Puponga beach, with the water of the bay and the island in the background.

Mike finished marking out the general composition of the painting and began to drop some azure blue into a section he had applied water to. This would be a background of sea. At a later stage he would apply other colours to provide the effect of wavelets and a distant horizon. Whilst he waited for the azure blue to dry he stepped out to observe the progress on the roof. Installation of the tiles seemed to be a stage of construction that marked the point when his house became more than just a structure. It was starting to look like a home . . . and a home that fitted in well with its environment. It was exciting to see this transition. Mike was admiring the colour of the tiles he had chosen when he heard a couple of vehicles slow down by his road frontage and then turn into Mereana's driveway. He recognised the distinctive crunching sound as they drove along her gravel driveway.

'I wonder who's visiting?' Mike thought. 'Perhaps Tamati? But why two vehicles?'

Mike started to feel a little concerned for Mereana and decided he needed to see what was happening. If he set out on his midday walk a little earlier than usual he could walk past and take a look.

On the road Mike walked slowly and glanced to his left. He was surprised to see a group of people sitting in plastic chairs arranged in a small circle on the scrubby lawn in front of the cabin. They seemed to be having a cup of tea. He saw that Tamati was there, sitting off to one side of Mereana. She seemed to be the centre of everyone's attention.

'Some kind of meeting going on,' he thought. 'Seems OK . . .'

Deciding to carry on with his walk Mike kept moving. Just then Mereana looked up and saw him. She startled everyone by suddenly getting to her feet and hurrying over to the front fence.

'Mike!' she called. 'Can I see you for a minute?'

Mike turned round and joined her at the fence. She looked very disconcerted.

'Sorry, Mike, but I have a huge favour to ask. Do you think you could meet my kaumatuas? Tamati has asked them to come to talk to me. I think they are going to try to get me to go back . . . You know how I feel about that . . . Anyway, I would feel a whole lot better if you could just be there . . . you know . . . to give me some moral support. I know I'll feel more confident in dealing with everything if you could just be with me . . . ?'

'Are you sure this is a good idea, Mereana? It seems like you're having some kind of family conference and I'm not family . . .'

'It is a bit like that, but you don't have to say anything.'

Mereana looked so anxious that Mike decided to agree.

'OK. If you think it would help, and if you just want me to sit and listen, I'm happy to do it.'

Looking obviously relieved Mereana said, 'Thanks so much, Mike . . . I'll introduce you and you'll have to hongi with them . . . I hope you don't mind that?'

'Fine by me, but I hope they won't feel I'm intruding in something that isn't my concern.'

'I'll explain why I invited you Mike, don't worry . . .'

As Mike approached the group he saw three elderly Maori women, an elderly Maori man and Tamati. He could tell by their frowns and raised eyebrows that these elders were, at the very least, surprised at his approach, and he could see that Tamati was very angry. As they arrived at the circle of chairs everyone rose and Mereana addressed them.

'I would like to introduce, Mike Robinson. Mike is building a house next door and he has helped me out a few times. We have become friends and I have found he is a very caring and wise person. I would like him to hear what is being said here today.'

There was a long pause when no one said anything. Then the older man cleared his throat and said, 'Kia ora, Mike. I will introduce myself and the others. I am Henare Whatarangi and Hepera, here, is my wife. To her left are Maria Kohe and Heni Waaka. Finally, we have Mereana's husband, Tamati. Tamati is lead negotiator for the claims we are preparing for the Waitangi Tribunal . . . and he is a leader at our marae. Tamati and Mereana recognise us as kaumatuas, elders if you like. Sometimes, when our young ones turn to us for advice, we can give them the benefit of our experience and knowledge of things Maori.'

Mike knew enough about Maori culture to know that he should now introduce himself and give them some idea of his background.

'Kia ora everyone. My name is Mike Robinson. As Mereana has explained, I live next door and I am building my house there. I am a retired engineer and I live alone now, having lost my wife in an accident some months ago. I have two adult children who live overseas. I was born in England, but I have lived in New Zealand for fifty-seven years and I am proud to call myself a New Zealander.'

Henare then approached Mike and shook his hand and pressed his nose to Mike's. The others formed up to hongi also. When it was Tamati's turn Mike saw a look of disdain in Tamati's expression. He wondered if Tamati had told anyone they had already met. Mereana then brought another chair into the circle and asked Mike to sit next to her.

When everyone was seated again there was an awkward pause before anyone spoke. Mike wondered who was going to break the silence. Eventually Henare Whatarangi looked at him quizzically and said, 'I suppose you must be wondering what this little gathering is all about, Mike? Or perhaps Mereana has given you some idea?'

'I assume you may be here to talk about Mereana's decision to take some time out, so she can consider her future.'

'Yes . . . well that's part of it anyway. Tamati is very unhappy that Mereana has taken 'time out' as you say. He wants Mereana to return to him and continue to be his wife. We kaumatuas were very surprised and concerned to learn that Mereana had suddenly decided to leave her husband, her home, and her position at the marae. She has always been a fantastic worker and role model for our younger folk and her skills as a teacher have been invaluable. Together, she and Tamati have achieved so much for our people . . . We have come here today, at Tamati's request, to see if there is anything we can do to help Mereana resolve whatever it is that caused this unexpected . . . difficulty. Now, I think it would be appropriate that we hear from Tamati.'

Tamati was obviously expecting this and he looked around the group as he gathered himself to speak.

'Tena koe. My position is very clear. I want Mereana to come back to me and our family. I want Mereana to return to her duties at the marae. I want her to be as she was before she decided to up stakes and come all the way here, to do God knows what, all on her own. I find it very hard to understand and accept that, after twenty years of marriage, Mereana can suddenly decide she doesn't want to stay married anymore . . . that she wants to leave me, leave the home we have made for made for our children, leave her job at Nayland College and abandon her work at the marae. She is turning her back on everything! This is wrong . . . and I worry how Matiu and Huia will react when they come home from their time overseas. I don't want them to return to a broken family. I have tried to get Mereana to see reason, but to no avail. So I thought it might help if she hears from her kaumatuas . . . about how much she is missed and how much she is needed by our people. I have swallowed my shame at what has happened and I am willing to make a new start with Mereana, if that's what it takes.'

Mike saw that Tamati had struggled to remain calm and speak in a controlled fashion, but he had noted the frustration and anger in his voice. He was sure the others would have recognised that too. Tamati's offer of making a new start didn't seem to sit well with the rest of his comments and, whilst he had been speaking, he had never once looked at Mereana. He certainly hadn't appealed to her directly to reconsider and come home.

Everyone turned their attention from Tamati to Henare, who seemed to be considering Tamati's remarks carefully. With a thoughtful glance at Tamati he turned to Mereana.

'Mereana, what do you have to say to us?'

Mereana leaned forward in her seat and calmly started to speak.

'Tena koutou. Firstly, I want to acknowledge and welcome your presence today . . . Haere mai . . . I certainly owe you an explanation for my decision to leave Nelson and come here . . . and I am pleased to have this opportunity to explain. I did not know I would be seeing you all today. When I received Henare's text message this morning I assumed that he was coming on his own. So this is all a bit of a surprise, but you are very welcome. It is good to see you. Haere mai!

'Tamati and I have worked together for the betterment of our people in Nelson for a long time now. We have always found great satisfaction in this and there have been some good times along the way. The two of us were thrown together, at a very young age, by a common cause. We believed in what we were doing. Later, when it was being suggested that we should marry we thought it was the right thing to do. Everyone expected it and some of you were . . . how should I say it . . . very encouraging at the time. It did not seem to be a big step from being good friends to being husband and wife, so we did it. As it happens our marriage did not turn out as I had expected. Of course we did have two wonderful children, and being married helped when it came to managing our work at the marae and so on, but I never ever felt as though our marriage was based on a foundation of love. It was more as if it was something we had to do and were expected to do . . . This is the way it has been . . . for most of our lives. Finally, when Matiu and Huia left to study overseas I realised that, as young adults, they would have less need of my time and guidance . . . and I knew that, when they return to New Zealand, they will be going away to university. For the first time I had some time to myself, time to think things over. Eventually I concluded I needed some time away from everything that was happening in Nelson to consider what to do with the rest of my life. I still had no feeling of fulfilment in my marriage to Tamati. He and I had . . . co-existed for so long . . . It had never been what I envisaged a loving relationship to be . . . It wasn't a bad life and I certainly don't hold Tamati to blame for the way I feel about this. We are both very proud of our children and I didn't want to do anything to break up our family when they were growing up, so I carried on. I imagine I felt much the way some of the Indian women do when they have entered into an arranged marriage. You don't have to love your husband to be a good wife and mother. But I have always wanted more. Maybe this has been selfish of me, but I cannot deny my feelings about this . . . and Tamati and I had become as ships that pass in the night . . . Over the past year we have seen very little of each other. Tamati's work has been all-consuming . . . I know how important the claim is, but for months on end he only came home to sleep.

'My life as Tamati's wife is now over . . . but I will always be a mother for Matiu and Huia . . . and I'll never give up my efforts to help our people. I don't know how I will continue this at the moment, but I will think of something. I would like to find some new ways to contribute . . . if I am granted the opportunity.'

Again there was silence as everyone digested Mereana's words. Mike gave her a quick nod and a smile. She was obviously anxious to hear some response. There was a stirring to Mike's left and he turned as Maria Kohe started to speak.

'I must say I find it quite upsetting to hear how unhappy Mereana has been . . . and of course Tamati is now unhappy also . . . I put up my hand and say that, yes, I was one of the ones who encouraged their marriage. I thought it was the right thing for them to do at the time and, goodness, I had no idea that Mereana had not been happy in her marriage! I think we should acknowledge how much they have both done to provide a welcoming place for everyone at the marae and how much they have done to help those who needed a hand up.

But perhaps all their time and effort for others has meant they have not had time for themselves . . . It does seem as though they have drifted apart and this is something I hate to see. I still think Tamati and Mereana can find happiness if they have the chance to work through this present situation.'

Heni Waaka then spoke up.

'I wonder if we haven't been remiss in not seeing what was going on under our noses. We have been so happy with everything we have seen these two doing for their people that we didn't see what was happening between them . . . or not happening . . . Tamati seems to be feeling anger and shame at what has happened and I can understand why he might feel angry . . . Men sometimes cannot accept that their wives seek to be . . . shall we say . . . independent. But he doesn't have to feel shame. Many marriages do not survive. This may be unfortunate, but it happens, and there should be no whakama . . . no shame in that. Mereana has said she never really loved Tamati and that their life together is at an end . . . She has taken a big step in leaving her husband, her job, and her work at the marae to come here to take time out. This is such a huge thing for her to decide and it seems to have happened very suddenly . . . I have the feeling that there might be more to all this than we have heard so far . . .'

'I think you are probably right, Heni,' Henare remarked. 'But we are not here to interrogate anyone and this is not a court case. Tamati asked us to help. He wanted us to see if we could persuade Mereana that she is badly missed and should come back to him and to us. Mereana has told us she needed time-out and I don't have a problem with that. Now, as a result of that time-out, she has decided her time with Tamati is over. I'm not sure I fully understand what convinces Mereana to say she and Tamati are finished, but I do take heart from her wish to continue to work for our people in some way. That means, to me, that we have not lost her completely.'

Clearly Tamati was not happy with the way things were proceeding. He had been squirming in his chair and looking very unhappy.

'I think a wife's place is alongside her husband. She has a duty to him and to her family. Mereana and I were chosen to become leaders in our community. I have certainly taken on this role and have worked very hard. She has worked hard too. Often this work has been at the expense of family time . . . I recognise that, but I don't accept this is a reason to end our marriage. And what is this love that Mereana talks about? I think love is different things to different people . . . We have been married for twenty years. It doesn't make sense to suddenly decide you aren't happy and throw it all away.'

Tamati looked at Mereana fiercely. His body language shouted anger and resentment and was evident to everyone.

'I did not suddenly throw everything away, as you say, Tamati. I have tried to talk to you a number of times about how I feel. But each time I tried you would not listen! You disregarded my feelings and you became very angry with me for daring to suggest that I wanted more than our marriage was providing. I do not feel the way you do about a woman's place in her marriage. Times have changed! Women no longer have to accept a subservient position and obey whatever their husband decides. I was unhappy and you wouldn't listen, and you wouldn't talk . . . and when you began to hit me it was time to call it quits!'

Mike heard at least two gasps of surprise at Mereana's last remark. Everyone turned to look at Tamati. He sat rigidly, his head down, avoiding any eye contact. It was obvious that Mereana had spoken the truth and Tamati had nothing to say in his defence.

Heni Waaka said, 'So now we have heard what it was that I sensed was being left unsaid before . . . I think this puts everything in a quite different light. Violence is no way to settle anything!'

Tamati looked as though he wanted to crawl under his seat.

Henare Whataroa sighed and looked around the group. No-one said anything. Tamati and Mereana were keeping their heads down. It seemed as though things had reached an impasse.

'Do you want to say anything, Mike?' Henare asked.

Mike wondered if he *should* say something. Then he looked at Mereana and saw her trembling and biting her lip. He realised she was struggling to hold herself together.

'Maybe I could just say that, in the brief time I have known Mereana, I have found her to be a very intelligent, mature and rational person. I don't think she does anything lightly. She thinks things through before she acts. She takes huge pride in her children, in her secondary school teaching and in her work at the marae. For her to leave her husband, and everything else, to come here to try to find a way through her problems must have taken great courage. The fact that you have all come here today, to try to get her back, reinforces my view that she means a great deal to your community. Mereana clearly does not accept Tamati's version of what her role should be in their marriage and to try to enforce his will by physically assaulting his wife is inexcusable to my way of thinking. I find that fact alone is sufficient reason for Mereana to take some time for reflection. Having done that, she has decided her marriage should end. This is something she must decide for herself and she obviously has. I don't know if it will be possible for Mereana and Tamati to find a way to be friends again, but not all marriages end with bitterness and disharmony . . . It is probably not my place to say, but it would be my suggestion that you all accept what Mereana has decided . . . and that she not become cast out from your community because of it. After many years of doing her best for others she is now looking for some kind of self-fulfilment. However, she still wants to support her people. I think she will need time, and your support, as she works out how this can be achieved in future.'

Henare looked impressed and was nodding his head.

'Kia ora, Mike . . . Your words make a lot of sense to me,' he said.

There were more expressions of 'kia ora' from the women and Mike felt the air of tension had suddenly dissipated. Mereana looked hugely relieved, but Tamati was looking very grim indeed. He suddenly got to his feet, glared furiously at Mike, ignored Mereana and everyone else and wordlessly stumped off to his car.

As he backed out and drove off Heni said, 'I really don't think anything else needs to be said!'

She and the others stood up and the meeting came to an end.

The three women each hugged Mereana and told her to take as much time as she needed to sort things out. Mike saw Heni Waaka shaking her head sadly as she and the other women made their way to their car. Henare then shook Mike's hand and spoke quietly.

'Looks like Mereana has found a very good friend in you, Mike. We had no idea Tamati had been hitting Mereana. That was truly shocking . . . Not acceptable at all . . . We'll obviously have to wait for Mereana to decide what she wants to do next, and we'll give her all the time and support she needs . . . . I'd better get going now, but it's been a pleasure meeting you . . .'

* * * * *

Mike hung back as Mereana walked to the roadside to wave goodbye to her kaumatuas. When they drove off she turned and ran back to him. She rushed up and flung her arms around him, giving him a fierce hug. He was so surprised he nearly fell.

'Thank you so much, Mike! When you spoke it made all the difference. Until then I didn't know what they were going to decide . . . You helped them deal with a difficult situation. They had obviously come here thinking that Tamati had been badly treated by me, and to talk some sense into me. It was only when they found out Tamati had been hitting me, and when you summed everything up so logically, that they realised their faith in Tamati had been misplaced. I'm so grateful you agreed to support me . . .'

Mike realised he was still holding Mereana in his arms . . . and it felt really good. As he let her go she said, 'Wow! Sorry, but that was kind of spontaneous . . . Hope you don't mind . . . ?'

Mike looked at her with raised eyebrows. She did look a little embarrassed, but she was smiling all the same.

'I'm all for spontaneity... Anyway, I think you have won over your kaumatuas. They will accept you won't be going back to Tamati and they certainly won't be casting you adrift as far as the Maori community is concerned. Tamati is a different kettle of fish though. If he thought he had lost some of his mana before, he has certainly lost a huge amount now. They are going to have some stern words with him, I'm picking, and I don't know if he is the kind of person who will accept what happened today without some kind of fight back. I'm worried he'll come back again . . .'

Mereana looked thoughtful.

'He will definitely never forgive me now, Mike. I have shown him up to be a wife-beater. This is something that is totally unacceptable. The marae has an anti-violence policy and we run anger management programmes to deal with this kind of thing. Tamati won't find it easy to regain his previous standing there, but I think they will want him to continue with the claim. After that . . . I don't know if he'll have the same respect . . . He took a gamble bringing the kaumatuas here and it turned out very badly for him. He won't forget what I did to him today and he will also hold a grudge against you I think, Mike.'

'That doesn't bother me, Mereana, although I would like to think it won't be quite as bad as you suggest . . . once the dust has settled and some time has gone by. If he is prepared to accept he was wrong to start hitting you, to prevent you from leaving him, it might be possible to have some kind of reconciliation . . . even if it's just for the sake of your children.'

'Maybe . . . I don't want us to be enemies and I don't want him to be your enemy either, but it will be up to him . . . He'll have to offer some kind of olive branch. I certainly don't feel I need to offer any compromises . . .'

'And you shouldn't. The ball is definitely in his court.'

'Come inside, Mike. I want to make lunch for you . . . Is that OK?'

'Sure. Lunch would be good.'

Over lunch Mike told Mereana how impressed he was with the way Henare and the women had handled things.

'You might be right in thinking they were coming to try to talk you into going back to Tamati and everything, but they weren't judgemental at all. If they had made up their minds that Tamati was the aggrieved party they certainly didn't show it. I liked the way they gave each of you the opportunity to talk and say anything you wanted to, and I was very surprised that I was invited to say something as well. Also, whenever anyone talked there was complete silence as we all listened. No-one interrupted or argued, not even Tamati. The whole thing was handled with dignity and it didn't take long. Once you had explained that Tamati had been hitting you I sensed that there was nothing more to be said really. They swung completely round to supporting you then, I think, even if they didn't say as much.'

'It was your summing up that was the clincher, Mike. You pointed out that I have not reacted irrationally and that I have the right to make my own decisions. It was that, together with the revelation of Tamati's violence towards me, which convinced them to let things be as they are. When we were saying goodbye each one of them made it clear they would give me whatever support they could. I felt vindicated and humbled . . . all at the same time.'

'What do you think Tamati will do now, Mereana?'

'I expect the kaumatuas will ask to see him in the next day or two. They'll talk to him about the inappropriateness of violence, and they'll probably suggest he accepts I've left him and that I need to go my own way now. They might suggest he apologises to me and tries to make amends somehow. I'm not sure about that, but they will probably want him to continue with everything he does at the marae . . . They will think he deserves to be given that chance . . . and, if he achieves a good settlement of our claims, that will give him the opportunity to regain his mana I think.'

'I hope you are right . . . and maybe someday he will stop seeing me as some kind of rival . . .'

Mereana looked at Mike sharply as he said that.

'What? Do you think he sees you as some kind of threat to him?'

'I'm not sure what he is thinking, but it is obvious he doesn't like the fact that I have come between the two of you . . . twice now . . . Maybe he thinks you and I are more than just neighbours and friends . . . which is ridiculous when you consider the difference in our ages . . .'

'I don't think it's so ridiculous, Mike,' Mereana said with a cheeky smile. 'Maybe I have a thing for older men! I certainly find you very attractive and how can I ignore the fact that you have come to my rescue so gallantly!'

Mike laughed.

'All right . . . That's enough of that nonsense! I think it's about time I went home to check how my roof is coming along.'

'OK, Mike. Perhaps you should do that before I say anything else to embarrass you!'

As Mike started for the door Mereana came up to him and hugged him again.

'This is my way of saying thanks again, Mike . . . I'll let you go now.'

As Mike walked back to his caravan he was smiling and felt a warm glow permeate his body. He shook his head.

'Silly old bugger!' he thought. 'That's just her way . . . Doesn't mean anything . . .'

Chapter 8.

When the roofer had finished his work Mike was able to start on the flooring, fixing sheets of MDF board to his floor joists. Once he had the floor down the glazier could install the glass doors and windows. This would be a two-day job and then Mike could begin to erect the internal partitions and a staircase, to provide access from the basement to the living area.

In the past few days Mike had seen Mereana only once, when she came in to tell him she was on her way to get some bread and milk from the grocery shop in Collingwood, the small settlement twenty minutes drive away. Mike had asked that she buy him some bread and milk also, plus a newspaper. That was all he needed before his next weekly trip to the supermarket in Takaka, the main town for the Golden Bay region, a forty minute journey by car.

When Mereana returned from Collingwood she put his purchases on the small table in his caravan and left him to continue his work uninterrupted. Mike had been thinking about Mereana, though, and he wondered how she was getting on with her writing. He assumed this was what she was doing most of the time. He was keen to spend more time with her, but felt he shouldn't be too obvious about it. He was worried about making a fool of himself. He wondered if she saw him as some kind of father figure, which would of course be perfectly natural given the twenty years difference in their ages, but he really hoped she didn't think that. He saw her as a very attractive woman, with a delightful personality and, despite himself, his feelings for her were becoming a whole lot more than neighbourly friendship . . . As he worked he would imagine what it would be like to be with her, hold her in his arms, love her . . . but then he would get really annoyed with himself for being so ridiculous. It was quite unrealistic to expect Mereana to feel anything towards him other than simple friendship, so he tried to put a rein on his fantasies and concentrate on his carpentry.

* * * * *

For her part, Mereana was enjoying having time to write and to go on exploration walks all around the area. She knew she was in a kind of limbo and would soon need to decide how she was going to live in future. She didn't have much money of her own left and would need to find a way to earn an income again. In the meantime, though, she was enjoying her newly won freedom.

As she walked out along the spit, or followed tracks to the various points of interest around Puponga, she would often think of Mike. She was confused by her attraction to him. She liked him a lot. He had been friendly and supportive and she respected the way he was starting to make a new life for himself after having lost his wife. But there had been a few times when she had felt some kind of chemistry between them, something that was definitely more than friendship, or respect. It had made her heart beat faster when she had felt it.

How could she feel this attraction to a much older person? He was actually not much younger than her father! Was this just some kind of crazy rebound thing, now that she had left Tamati after twenty years of marriage? Had she fixed on the first man who had come along after she realised she could actually consider new relationships?

'This is probably all a bit crazy,' she said to herself. 'But I definitely feel I want to be with him more and get to know him better. He says he enjoys my company, but that could just be that he's a really nice person. Then again, I think he might have felt the same chemistry thing as me. There have been two or three times when I'm sure we both felt it. Something was happening to us and I don't think it was just my imagination . . .'

Mereana also thought about Mike as a pakeha. She had been immersed in things Maori all her life. Her husband, children and best friends were all Maori. The people she looked to for advice and guidance had always been Maori. She felt deeply in tune with her Maori heritage and culture. What would it be like to become involved with someone from such a different background and life experience? Of course there had always been a great deal of intermarriage in New Zealand, to the extent that there were probably no living Maori without some mixed ethnicity within their family histories. This was the way of the world now and it was inevitable. Her own genealogy included instances where Maori ancestors had married pakeha women, but she had always considered herself Maori ahead of anything else. Although she lived and worked within a modern multi-cultural society and fully understood and accepted the differences of history and culture among the New Zealand population, she had always preferred to be guided in her own life by Maori values. Could a pakeha man ever fully accept her on this basis? Because she would never compromise those values.

Mereana also tried to think how Matiu and Huia would cope with her decision to leave their father. She hoped they would be mature enough to understand that she wanted more from life, now that she had reviewed her situation and stepped away from her marriage. She intended to talk to them about it very soon now. They would be shocked of course and it might be hard for them to understand why she felt she needed to move on, particularly as she had decided not to mention that their father had been physically abusive. In the end, though, they would be faced with a fait accompli. All she could do was hope they wouldn't resent her actions and become estranged from her. Actually, she was reasonably confident they would accept what she had done, but she was a lot less sure what they would think if she took up with another man, especially if he was a lot older and a pakeha! But the more Mereana thought about Mike the more she was determined not to hold back on the way she felt about him. This was her new life now and she didn't want to feel constrained by what others might think. Having come to that resolution Mereana decided to take the initiative and go to see Mike.

* * * * *

After working hard all day on his flooring Mike was pleased to knock off and head back to his caravan for a shower. He decided to put on clean clothes and take a bottle of wine next door, to see if Mereana wanted to have a drink or two with him before dinner.

Taking a bottle of Kim Crawford riesling from his fridge he headed off. As he stepped onto the road he stopped and laughed. Mereana was coming towards him, also carrying a bottle of wine!

'I can't believe this!' Mereana said with a huge grin.

'Neither can I, but they say great minds think alike.'

'Well . . . what do we do now, Mike? Will it be your place or mine?'

'Hmm . . . I'd offer to toss you for it, but methinks there may be a tad more room in your cabin. My caravan is definitely space challenged . . .'

'Yes, but it's cosy and it's intimate . . . wouldn't you say?

'Your place is too! And I'll bet it's a lot more tidy than mine . . .'

'Oh, all right then. Let's decide on my place.'

'Agreed!'

Mereana stepped up and hooked her arm through Mike's and, together, they walked to the cabin.

Mereana looked up at Mike with a cheeky grin.

'What would the kaumatuas say if they could see us now, I wonder?'

Mike tried to think of a suitable response.

'They would probably think that you are being a bit reckless with your newfound freedom and that, at my age, I should know better than to encourage you . . .'

'Well they can think that if they like. I don't care! We can enjoy each other's company if we want to . . .'

As he opened the front door for Mereana, Mike said, 'We're both agreed on that then!'

CHAPTER 9.

The next day Mereana decided to explore the track leading to one of the old worked-out coal mines. The day was grey and damp, with very low cloud cover, the softest of breezes and a fine misty drizzle saturating everything. This type of weather kept most people indoors, but Mereana enjoyed walking in the rain. She wore a softball cap, jeans, a dark green anorak and sturdy walking shoes.

The track passed through mature kanuka trees. In the early 1900's it was the route of a railway, built to carry coal from the mine to the wharf. A small steam locomotive was used to shunt wagons, each carrying a tonne of coal, to the waiting ships. At the end of the wharf, where the ships were waiting, the wagons were tipped sideways to spill the coal down chutes and into the ship's hold. Now, the rails had been removed and the track was quite narrow and overgrown, with ferns and flaxes almost blocking it in parts. In some places kanuka trees were overhanging to provide a dense canopy. There was a distinct smell of rotting vegetation. Mereana noticed signs that a vehicle had recently passed along the track and she wondered who would want to drive to up to the old mine. The track was hardly serviceable and in places a vehicle would have had to push through the encroaching vegetation.

As she walked Mereana reflected on the previous evening. She and Mike enjoyed the riesling and then she had persuaded him to stay on for dinner. She had already cooked a steak and kidney pie, so it had been easy to heat this up and add some green beans and carrots. She was sure Mike had enjoyed himself and the food she had prepared. There had been no sparks of chemistry between them this time, but they had talked about all sorts of things and felt very relaxed in each other's company. Over dinner they had moved on to Mereana's cabernet sauvignon and, by the time they had finished that, they were both feeling decidedly mellow. Mike had eventually decided he should head off back to his caravan, but it had been obvious he was reluctant to bring their evening together to a close. Mereana had given him a quick peck on the cheek as he headed out the door, and he had given her a quick hug as he said goodbye and hoped she would sleep well.

'We did have a good time together,' she thought. 'He's such a lovely man . . .'

As Mereana progressed along the track the deep silence was occasionally punctuated by the call of a tui, or bellbird. It could sometimes be hard to tell which. She saw plenty of the little silvereyes flitting from branch to branch, but when she saw a pair of fantails she stopped to watch them flutter about, making their high pitched tweets and doing their best to flush out an insect or two. Fantails fascinated her and she loved to watch their agility in the air. As this pair moved away from the track and darted from one kanuka tree to the next Mereana followed, picking her way between tree-trunks, tree ferns and fallen branches. The ground was spongy underfoot, with a thick coating of tiny leaves that looked like English tea. The fantails were obviously a breeding pair. Although they were hunting separately they always seemed to be aware where their mate was and did not stray too far apart. Suddenly, Mereana found herself at the edge of a clearing. It was an area about thirty metres long and twenty metres wide, totally surrounded by kanuka. As she moved out from under the trees, to see what was growing in the clearing, she stumbled over a tight-drawn string and heard a sudden clanking noise off in the distance.

Realisation came to her in a rush! She had obviously stumbled upon a patch of cannabis plants . . . and she had tripped over the growers' alarm system!

'Oh my God!' she thought, as she turned to run as quickly as she could back to the track. She had heard of this sort of thing. It was strictly illegal to grow cannabis, so the criminals involved would often conceal their activities by planting their crop in out-of-the-way places, usually in forested, or scrub covered areas where they would be hard to detect, even from helicopters. Mereana knew the Police conducted helicopter searches for hidden cannabis plots from time to time and she had heard they had been successful in finding quite a bit in the Golden Bay area. The growers tried to protect their crops by rigging up alarm systems and even barricades. It was not unknown for rival cannabis growers to poach from each other, especially when a crop was ready for harvest, and Mereana had read that serious fights between rival growers and dealers were not uncommon.

She walked back down the track as fast as she could, but soon heard the sound of a vehicle approaching from behind. She decided to slip into the undergrowth beside the track and hide out until the vehicle passed. She pressed into a large clump of flax and crouched down. Her heart was pounding and she felt very frightened. As the vehicle, a Toyota Hilux Ute, drove past she saw three men in the cab. They were staring ahead intently, obviously trying to locate whoever had found their cannabis patch. Mereana waited motionless for another five minutes before deciding to move back to the track and cautiously make her way back to the road. She heard and saw nothing and began to think she was in the clear until she emerged from the track. The Ute was parked about fifty metres back along the road and she could see the men inside looking in her direction.

'Oh my God! What do I do now?' she wondered, with a surge of alarm.

Mereana did her best to act unconcerned, as though nothing had happened. She forced herself not to run and walked off towards home as fast as she could.

After a few minutes she risked a look back. Damn! There was a man following her on foot! He was about sixty metres back. All Mereana could do was to keep going and hope she could get home in time and lock her doors. Whenever Mereana glanced back the man was there, keeping his distance, matching her pace.

'Should I go back to the cabin? If I do he'll know where I live! Should I go straight to Mike? If I do that I could be causing big trouble for him! . . . Maybe they'll think I'm no threat to them . . . just a local wandering around. They might even think I don't realise what they have been doing. Some chance of that! They wouldn't be that naïve . . . Oh God, what should I do?'

In the end, Mereana decided to continue her pretence of normality and to make for the cabin. The man seemed prepared to keep his distance. He could easily have caught up with her if he had wanted to. She thought she would be safe enough in the cabin and, when she was sure the man had returned to his friends, she would go next door to ask Mike what she should do.

* * * * *

Just as he finished laying the last sheet of MDF board, to complete his flooring, Mereana popped her head up through the gap that would one day contain the stairwell. She had climbed the ladder Mike had been using to get up and down. He could tell she was very worried about something. She looked really agitated.

'Mike, I had to come over . . . I'm really worried. I'm wondering if I should be going to see the Police in Takaka . . .'

'What's happened? Is it Tamati?'

'No. Not Tamati . . . but I think I might have stirred up a hornet's nest, Mike, and I don't know what to do for the best . . .'

As Mereana explained what had happened Mike became very concerned.

'They followed you all the way home?'

'Yes. Well, one of them did. I didn't see the others, or the Ute, again.'

'Hmm. I think we had better assume that they are not going to ignore the fact that you have seen their operation, Mereana. They'll have a lot riding on that cannabis crop and they won't want you telling anyone about it . . . Look,

I'm going to knock off now. I think we should go straight to Takaka to report this and ask them what they will do about it. Is that OK with you?'

'I'm sure you're right, Mike. I wouldn't feel safe in the cabin now, knowing they could appear at any time.'

'I don't blame you. There have been some reports about some of these cannabis dealers getting quite nasty if they feel they, or their cannabis is threatened. There is such big money tied up in it all that they can be quite ruthless in protecting their um . . . investment.'

Mereana followed Mike to the caravan and, when he reached for some clothes, she realised he was about to strip off and get changed.

'Um . . . I'll just step outside, Mike . . .'

Mike looked at her with a grin.

'Up to you . . . but you don't need to and it *is* raining. I'm not going to get totally naked! I'm sure you can stand seeing me in my underwear, although it's not a pretty sight!'

'I want to get changed too, Mike. My jeans are really wet and my shoes are soaked. I'll just pop next door. I'll only be a couple of minutes.'

'No! That's definitely not a good idea. Look I'm nearly ready . . . Just bear with me for a moment and I'll go over there with you. You definitely shouldn't be on your own at the moment.'

'All right then . . . I promise I'm trying not to look . . . but those blue boxers look pretty sexy!'

'Arrh . . . you're just saying that!'

* * * * *

An hour later they were being interviewed by Barry Sanders, the Sergeant in charge at the Takaka Police Station. Mereana told him her story, step by step, and was then asked to indicate, on a topographical map, exactly where the cannabis was growing.

'All right, Mrs Marshall. Thank you for coming in straight away. I'll get right on to organising a raid. With a bit of luck those characters will still be around, but even if we miss them we'll probably be able to seize their crop. If there are three of them it seems they may be about to start harvesting. From what you said about the size of the plants that would seem quite possible. We need to move quickly, because now they know you have rumbled them they'll more than likely have started to harvest the stuff. They'll be working flat out I should think.'

'When do you think you'll be able to get your team up there?' Mike asked.

'Oh, I should think we'll be there early in the morning. I'll report this to the CIB Drug Intelligence boys in Nelson right away. They'll probably bring a team over. We'll have a better chance of apprehending whoever is there if we have a full crew on the job. It is short notice, but it sounds like there's a sizeable crop involved and I think CIB will want to move in as quickly as possible . . . Now, in the meantime, I don't want you going anywhere near that cannabis and you shouldn't go back to your place tonight, Mrs Marshall. They may be on the lookout for you there. Is there anywhere else you can go until we move in?'

Mike quickly responded.

'She can stay with me if she likes. I'll make sure she's safe.'

Mereana looked intently at Mike. She was really surprised. She had been thinking she would probably need to stay in Takaka.

'You sure, Mike? I could easily stay at a motel here in Takaka . . . ?

'Well, that's up to you and, if you decide that way, I'll be happy to come back for you tomorrow after the Police have done their stuff . . . But you are welcome to stay with me . . . if you want.'

They both knew that this was a significant decision. The caravan was basically just a one room affair, with one bed, only a little larger than a single. It did have a separate shower/toilet, but apart from that there was no chance of any privacy.

Mike was deliberately not looking at Mereana as she thought about it. She instantly knew what she wanted to do and she couldn't help feeling a thrill of anticipation.

'Well, I'm not sure . . . but if you really don't mind, I do think I would feel better if I was not on my own . . . I will need to get a couple of things from the cabin though.'

'If that's really necessary I think Mike should be with you when you do that,' the Sergeant said. 'You'll need to be careful there's no-one waiting for you. There probably won't be though. I'm guessing those men have more than enough to do, harvesting their crop and then getting out of there . . . but you never know. If it looks all clear you should get your things as quickly as you can and leave. You'll need to keep yourselves well out of sight until I give you the word that we've apprehended these people. Anyway, thanks again for letting us know what's going on up there. I'll come and see you once we've wrapped everything up tomorrow. We'll need to get a formal statement from you, Mrs Marshall . . . and we may also need you to give evidence in a month or two, when the case comes to trial.'

*****

As they left the Police Station Mike turned to Mereana.

'Look, Mereana . . . What I said in there . . . about you staying over with me tonight. It just slipped out . . . Perhaps your idea of staying in a motel here tonight would be best . . . Having the two of us stay in the caravan is probably . . . um . . . a bit inappropriate . . . and I didn't mean to embarrass you . . .'

Mereana gave Mike a wry grin and said, 'Let's get in the car shall we?'

In the car Mereana leaned across and put her arms around Mike's neck and kissed him lightly on the cheek.

'I do want to stay with you tonight, Mike. I don't know about it being inappropriate . . . it doesn't seem that way to me really, but perhaps others would think so. Anyway, they don't need to know and it's none of their business! I'm game if you are . . .'

'I don't care what other people think, Mereana. I just don't want *you* to think I'm being insensitive, or ridiculous . . . The caravan isn't really suitable is it? I mean there's no way we can . . .'

Mereana interrupted.

'Mike! I know what the caravan's like. And I don't think you are insensitive, or ridiculous. I don't want to be by myself tonight . . . I do want to be with you . . . Is that OK?'

Mereana was looking quite demure and a little flushed as she said this and Mike thought how very desirable she looked. He wondered if he was looking as embarrassed and sheepish as he felt.

'All right . . . If you're sure, it will be my pleasure . . .'

Mereana hugged him again and murmured, 'Can we go now, Mike?'

'Right . . . Seeing we're in Takaka I would like to get some eggs and bacon and a couple of bottles of wine. I'd also like to call in to the depot at Collingwood on the way back. I have a parcel of nails and screws and things to pick up from there. Maybe we could have a coffee there too?'

*****

By the time they arrived back at Puponga the sun was setting. Mike drove straight up to the caravan and asked Mereana to wait inside it.

'I'll just take a look next door. If it looks like the coast is clear I'll come back for you and we can go over to get whatever you need.'

Rather than walking out onto the road and then down Mereana's driveway Mike decided to climb the fence that ran between the two properties and approach from the rear. He was careful to check that no-one was in sight before he straddled the fence and dropped to the other side. Then, following the line of the fence and keeping under the cover of manuka trees, he approached the cabin. He saw no-one. After a quick circuit of the cabin he carried on out to the road and carefully looked both ways to see if anyone was laying in wait. As far as he could tell there was no-one and there were no vehicles parked along the road either.

On his return to the caravan Mike said, 'I think it's safe for you to get your things, Mereana. Let's go over now. We'll need to be as quick as we can.'

Mike led the way and opened the front door. Immediately they were assailed by a very strong stench of decomposed flesh. The smell was almost overpowering.

'God that's foul! What is it? Whew!' Mike exclaimed. 'Just hold back a minute, I'd better go first and see what it is.'

Inside Mike quickly discovered the source of the awful stink.

'Oh my Lord! That is so gross!' he cried. 'You'd better take a quick look, Mereana. Your drug dealers have left a message for you!'

Mereana cautiously came through the door and gasped when she saw what was on her dining table. It was the rotting remains of a dead sheep. Its stomach had been sliced open and its entrails had disgorged over the table and down onto the floor. The innards were covered in a seething mass of maggots and the stench of putrefaction was quickly making her feel very sick. On a piece of cardboard propped next to the carcass a crude message had been scrawled in block letters.

'SAY NOTHING BITCH OR THIS COULD HAPPEN TO YOU'

Mereana began to feel very frightened. She couldn't speak and was so horrified that she clutched at Mike for support. Whereas she had paled in shock, he was livid with anger.

'Get your things, Mereana, and we'll get out of here. The Police need to see this, so we'll have to leave it like it is for now. The bastards! They can't be allowed to get away with this type of intimidation. It's totally unacceptable! They need to be put away for a very long time!'

CHAPTER 10.

Back in the caravan Mike said, 'I think we need a drink, don't you? How about a small tot of whisky?'

Mereana was sitting and leaning on the little table, trying to control her shaking.

'God! That was awful, Mike! I never guessed they'd do anything like that! I'm feeling quite sick . . . and that poor sheep!'

'It had been dead for a while, Mereana, and they obviously thought they could use it to frighten you off. Makes me think they must be a pretty desperate. They were too late, though, weren't they! They must have turned up with the sheep just when you were reporting them . . . I reckon they'll be going hell for leather right now, cutting down all their plants. I just hope the cops get there before they've loaded up and left the place . . . I'd really like to go and see what they are doing . . .'

'Don't you even think of it, Mike! I don't want you to go anywhere right now. We'll just have to put our faith in Sergeant Sanders and his team, and wait until the morning to hear something.'

'Yeah . . . You're right . . . but it's frustrating having to wait, knowing they could get away.'

'From what I saw they wouldn't be able to harvest all those plants quickly. They'll have to spend hours and hours on it. So, unless they are prepared to abandon it all, they'll still be there I think.'

'Probably going to work through the night. I doubt they'll be prepared to just leave it . . . too much money at stake . . . Let's just hope they are greedy enough to keep working until the Police get there.'

'Yes! And let's hope they think their little message to me has kept me quiet!'

'I'll drink to that, Mereana!'

* * * * *

Mike opened a bottle of Pinot Noir to have with a meal of porterhouse steak, onions, sweet corn, potatoes and peas. Mereana insisted on being the cook, but afterwards they washed and dried the dishes together. Their conversation had steered away from the drug dealers, but they were never far from their minds. Mereana was keen to know how Mike was going to proceed with his new house and this kept them talking for an hour. Mike then set up his small TV set and they found a travel programme to watch. As the presenter extolled the wonders of Vietnam as a holiday location neither of them was really focused on the programme. They were both thinking about the fact that they would be spending the night together and about their sleeping arrangements.

After a while Mereana said, 'Mike, how are we going to do this tonight? I think we're both feeling a bit awkward about it now aren't we?'

'That's very perceptive of you! I *have* been wondering how to broach the subject . . . What do you think? I can probably arrange things so we each have our own sheets and blankets . . .'

'That's fine with me, if you want to do it that way . . . but don't you think that's going to be a bit awkward? There's not much room for two separate sleeping arrangements is there?'

'I was just trying to work out a way to respect your modesty, or dignity, I suppose. The other alternative is that we sleep together . . . maybe top and tail . . .'

'I'm sure we are mature enough to sleep together normally . . . I can cope with that . . . I'm not expecting you to force yourself upon me or anything . . .'

'That would be the last thing I'd do . . . I want to nurture our friendship, not destroy it! I'm not the sort of person who would do something like that.'

'I know it . . . and I'm all for that nurturing thing, Mike. In fact it sounds wonderful . . . so nurture away!'

'Fair enough! . . . I'll make up the bed then shall I?'

* * * * *

As Mike set up the bed Mereana slipped into the shower/toilet to clean her teeth and change into her nightwear. Then, after a moment of hesitation, she sprayed a little perfume on her throat. She knew full well that she was trying to make herself more desirable and she felt a flutter of arousal. When Mike called out that the bed was ready she stepped out in a blue silk nightdress. The sight of Mereana in a rather clinging nightdress and looking a little flushed took Mike's breath away.

'Wow! Don't you look a sight for sore eyes!' he said. 'I might have to reneg on my promise to be a good boy!'

Mereana's eyes sparkled and she grinned shyly as she got into the bed.

'Keep the compliments coming, Mike. I'll take all I can get! Your turn to use the bathroom I think.'

Mike's baggy flannel pyjamas had nothing like the allure of Mereana's choice of nightwear and, when he emerged from the shower/toilet, Mereana laughed and whistled appreciatively.

'You'll have to excuse these,' Mike said. 'These pyjamas have definitely seen better days . . . I don't usually wear them.'

'You mean I'm missing out on seeing you in the buff?'

'You are, but it's all for the best don't you think?'

'Definitely! I don't know what I'd have done if you hadn't worn them!'

'Probably run home, screaming, I'd imagine . . .'

'Oh, I would have been really shocked, but I doubt I'd have screamed, or made a run for it. I don't really know what I would have done . . .'

'Well you don't have to make that decision . . . Just as well I had something to wear! Hardly as sexy as what you're wearing though! I'll get in beside you now and I'll put a pillow between us, so I don't roll over to your side.'

'Mike! For goodness sake! There's hardly room for the two of us let alone an extra pillow! You can stop trying to protect my virtue this minute! . . . I mean it! I'm a big girl now!'

With that Mereana reached over and pulled Mike into her arms. Mike tentatively put his arms around her, but he felt stiff and awkward.

'Relax, Mike . . . It's OK . . . This feels right to me. I want it to be right for you too . . .'

'I'm sorry . . . It's not that I don't want to hold you or anything . . . Quite the opposite, but I don't seem to be able to get over the fact that this is happening and you and I are . . . you know . . . And I must admit I'm feeling a little guilty . . . It's less than six months since Rosie died . . .'

Mike felt Mereana stiffen as he mentioned Rosie and she gently pulled away from him and rolled away.

'Look . . . sorry . . . I shouldn't have said that, Mereana. That is my problem not yours . . . The truth is that I want you here with me more than anything . . . It's just that my stupid conscience is getting in the way . . .'

'I understand, Mike. What you said made me feel guilty too. You are trying to be true to your wife . . . even when she is gone now . . . You obviously loved her very much. You must think I'm terrible . . . because I'm still married for goodness sake!'

'I certainly *don't* think you are terrible! You might still be technically married, but as far as I can see the marriage is over . . . I don't think you should feel any kind of guilt . . . I respect you tremendously for your decision to leave Tamati. I think you made a truly courageous decision . . . and you had every right to leave . . .'

'Well neither should you feel terrible, Mike. You obviously loved Rosie very much, but you've said it yourself . . . you are trying to make a fresh start and move on with your life now. I don't think you will dishonour Rosie if you start a new relationship, and I don't think Rosie would want you to feel inhibited and not able to do what you want to do . . . I'm sure she would want you to be happy and for you to feel free to do whatever it takes to achieve that happiness.'

Mike lay on his back thinking about what Mereana had said. She was absolutely right of course. It was just that he was finding it difficult to come to terms with it all. He wanted Mereana. He was amazed that she seemed to want him! It was wonderful! He decided he needed to get over himself . . . He turned to Mereana and pulled her to him.

'You are a very wise woman, Mereana. I'm being an idiot. Please forgive me. I love having you with me like this . . .'

'Perhaps it's all happening a bit too fast, Mike . . . You know, I wouldn't be here now if it wasn't for those damned cannabis people. But I do think we have both been feeling something special about each other . . . You are right about Tamati. I did make the right decision to leave him and I have to move on, just like you do . . . So I'm not ashamed to be here like this with you . . .'

Mike gently pulled her by the shoulder and she turned to face him.

'Let's not talk any more then . . . Let's accept that this has happened to us . . . It wasn't what we planned, but it's what we both want . . . very much.'

Mike leaned forward to kiss Mereana and she responded eagerly. They held each other tightly and their kisses became more and more passionate.

'Wow!' Mereana exclaimed as they came up for breath. 'That was lovely! It feels so right! You're a great kisser . . . and I want more!'

'Come on then, but I'm not sure if I'll be able to restrain myself . . .'

The time for talk was clearly over. Their kisses were just a prelude as they both gave in to their desire for each other . . .

* * * * *

Mike was the first to wake. He looked across at Mereana and saw she was still sound asleep, facing him with one arm across his waist. He immediately thought about their lovemaking and felt himself stir again. She looked innocent and very beautiful, laying there with her raven black hair spread around the pillow, framing her face. He gently lifted her arm and slid out of the bed. He was mildly surprised to find he was naked . . . but then he remembered and smiled.

The sound of the toilet flushing woke Mereana and she looked up to see Mike getting dressed.

'Good morning lovely man.' she said.

'Good morning to you too! I thought I'd better get up, because otherwise I might have been tempted to keep you in bed all day! And we might need to talk to the Police soon.'

'What time is it?'

'It's nearly 7.00 . . . How about I make a cup of tea? You can have it in bed.'

'No. I'm going to get up too. I want to be ready in case things start to happen. Have you heard any cars go by, or anything?'

'Nothing so far, but things are probably going to start happening shortly if Barry Sanders has managed to get his team together.'

'OK, I'm up!'

Mereana threw aside the bedclothes and stood up. In one step she was hugging Mike and he gasped as she moulded her naked body to his. Mereana quickly kissed him on the lips and then grabbed some clothes and slipped into the shower/toilet. Mike shook his head. He was feeling astonished, amazed and just happy . . . very happy.

'How good is this?' he thought.

Chapter 11.

After Mike had finished laying the internal floors of his new house he turned his attention to the main outside job. This was laying the decking timber and erecting the balustrade. He was using a hardwood called kwila for the deck. It needed to be cut to size and holes for screws that would secure the planks to the floor joists had to be drilled. Mereana had volunteered to help and, after having a quick breakfast, they made an early start. Mike found it was much easier to cut the long planks to size when Mereana held and steadied one end as he operated the draw saw. Then, once the plank was set and clamped in place, she could drill the screw holes, using a battery-powered drill, and he could follow on behind to drive in the screws.

As they worked they kept an ear cocked for signs of activity on the road. Initially they heard nothing and by 8.15am they were starting to think that the Police might be leaving it too late. Just then, however, a helicopter flew over, about two hundred metres up. It flew in a straight line and continued out of sight, seemingly a scenic flight along Farewell Spit. A few minutes later a police patrol car quietly drove in and stopped alongside the caravan.

Barry Sanders and a policewoman got out of the car Mereana and Mike climbed down the ladder and went to meet their visitors.

'Morning!' said Barry. 'This is Penny McKay. The rest of the team is waiting just down the road. We are about ready to go in . . . I assume you've been all right?'

'Um . . . Not exactly,' Mereana replied. 'They got into my cabin and left a very unpleasant surprise, a dead sheep, and a warning that I should say nothing. We left it all just as we found it, so you can see it for yourself . . . It's pretty unpleasant . . .'

'So they tried to frighten you into silence?'

'They certainly did, but we had already talked to you anyway. They would have broken in when we were seeing you in Takaka.'

'Right, well, we'll certainly take a look, but right now we are about to move in on these guys. The CIB arranged for a helicopter to fly over a few minutes ago and we've had radio contact with it. The pilot reported signs of activity up by the old mine where you saw the cannabis patch. Apparently they have two vehicles and it looks as if they are in the process of loading them up. I'll come back and see you after we've done our stuff and then you can show me what happened next door. OK?'

'Fine by us,' Mike said. 'Good luck!'

'Thanks . . . Oh, and by the way, I hope you weren't planning on going out for a while . . . We have set up a roadblock, about three hundred metres from here, just in case they try to make a run for it. No-one will be able to get through for a while.'

'That won't bother us. We're going to be staying here,' Mereana responded.

Barry nodded and spoke into his mobile radio.

'TCR 1 to TCR 2 . . .'

'Two receiving . . .'

'Let the Nelson boys know we're good to go as planned, Jeff. Let's go get them!'

Within seconds three vehicles accelerated along the road and Barry Sanders and Penny McKay got into their car and turned out of the driveway to follow.

'Let's hope they can catch them all red-handed,' Mike said. 'They'll be there in about five minutes I reckon.'

A short while later they heard the sound of the helicopter again. They looked up to see it approaching rapidly from along the spit and then drop down to hover about sixty metres above the ground.

'Looks like it's directly over the cannabis patch,' Mereana exclaimed.

'They'll be making sure no-one does a runner I think,' Mike said. 'If anyone tries to make their escape the helicopter will be able to track them and direct the guys on the ground to where they are.'

'It's quite exciting isn't it! I hope they go quietly and no-one gets hurt . . . What are we going to do with that sheep, Mike?'

'I think I'll dig a big hole and, once Barry Sanders has had a look at it, I'll bury it. I expect he'll want to take some photos for evidence . . .'

* * * * *

After about twenty minutes they saw the helicopter head away towards Takaka and about ten minutes later Mereana heard sounds of vehicles approaching. As she and Mike looked out from the deck they saw a patrol car and a police van drive by. Then another half hour went by before Barry Sanders and Penny McKay returned with another policeman.

'How did it go?' Mike asked as they pulled up next to the caravan and got out of the patrol car.

'Like a dream! This is Garry Palmer by the way. He's with Nelson CIB. Mrs Marshall is the lady who reported what was going on, Garry.'

Mike and Mereana shook hands with the man.

'I'll let Garry tell you what happened,' Barry said.

'It's been a really good result!' Garry said enthusiastically. 'And that's because of your information, Mrs Marshall . . . They had just finished loading and were about to leave when we drove up the track and blocked them in. They looked ready to make a run for it until they saw the helicopter arrive. That's when they seemed to accept they were done for. Lucky they weren't armed, so that made things a bit easier. Anyway, they didn't resist arrest. There were three of them and they're on their way to the station now. We recognised them straight away. They are from Motueka and they're pretty tough characters, well known in the local drug scene. They have been nabbed doing this sort of thing before . . . Their last patch was up in the Motueka valley, near the river. They'll be serving a good stretch this time . . . There's not much leniency for repeat offenders.'

'We saw the paddy wagon go by,' Mike said.

'Yes, they'll go straight to Motueka in that and be put in the cells there for the meantime. The three we caught all work for another villain, a guy called Kenny McCann. He is well known as the number one dealer in the region, but we've been unable to get enough evidence to put him away as yet. I think he must be pretty ruthless, because, so far, no-one who has worked for him, and been caught, has been prepared to put the finger on him . . . They are way too frightened.

'We've seized their vehicles and all the cannabis. I've still got some lads at the scene, gathering evidence and taking photos. Your tip-off was only just in time, by the way. They had a mature crop and they'd have been gone later today if you hadn't alerted us.'

'We thought they might have been harvesting through the night,' Mereana said.

'Hmm . . . Probably . . . That might explain why they looked so knackered when we arrested them . . . Anyway, it's a great result for us and it's all thanks to you. Now, Penny can stay by the radio whilst Barry and I take a look next door. I understand you had a break-in . . .'

Barry took one look at the rotting sheep's carcass and the warning message and backed out of the cabin. He had a disgusted look on his face. Garry then emerged from the cabin looking grim and said, 'That's nasty! I'll have to get our photographer to record that little lot. Should be at least two more charges for them to face, if we can find the forensics to link it to them . . . Can't have been nice for you to come home to that, Mrs Marshall! Look, once the boys have finished dusting for prints and taking photos I'll have them remove the sheep. If we can get a hole dug somewhere I'll get the lads to tidy it away as best they can. Might not be until later in the day though. They'll be busy up at the cannabis patch for quite a while yet.'

'I'd already decided to dig a big hole, so I'll get on to that. In the meantime, if you or your team want to come back here for a break at any time, we'd be glad to provide a cup of tea or coffee.' Mike offered.

'That's kind. We'll probably take you up on that!'

Mereana asked, 'Do you think they will be granted bail until their case is heard? I'm worried they might come back here to exact some kind of retribution. They'll know it was me that reported them . . .'

'We'll be opposing bail, because of their previous convictions and because they have threatened you,' Garry replied. 'I'm pretty sure that will be enough to convince a Judge to keep them locked up. I can't guarantee it though. If they do get bail I'll be sure to let you know. Now, Barry and I will head back to see how the boys are getting on back up by the mine and we'll leave Penny with you, to take your statement. She'll type it up once she gets back to the station and you'll need to drop by to sign it in the next day or two. Is that OK?'

'Sure,' Mereana replied.

CHAPTER 12.

It took Mereana ages to clean up the dining table and floor in the cabin. The police team had removed as much as they could of the stinking carcass, but the smell remained and pervaded the whole cabin. Mereana sprayed air freshener everywhere, but it was obviously going to take time for the odour of putrefaction to dissipate. Having done the best she could Mereana decided she needed to tell Matiu and Huia about her decision to leave their father. She had been putting it off for too long and needed to send text messages to ask them to advise a time when she could call them.

Cell phone coverage at Puponga was always marginal and, if a signal could be obtained, it was almost always at the lowest end of the range. Mereana had found that walking across the road to the beach often provided some reception, whereas reception at the cabin seemed to come and go inexplicably.

From the beach Mereana could hear Mike at work. It sounded like he was moving timber around. She decided to go and see how he was getting on after she had sent her text messages. Turning her cell phone on she found she had two unread messages, one from Matiu and the other from Huia.

* * * * *

Mike was hauling some more kwila planks up to the part-finished deck when Mereana come through the gate. He immediately saw, from her body language, that she was quite agitated. He decided to climb down the ladder and find out what was wrong.

'Manage to clean up the cabin OK, Mereana?'

'As best I can for now. It's going to take a while for the smell to go though.'

'Good! That means you should stay with me again tonight, doesn't it?'

'If that's all right with you,' Mereana said distractedly. 'Look Mike, I've just heard from the kids. I'm really worried . . . They are both on their way home!'

Mike realised that this was a big surprise to Mereana. No wonder she had seemed agitated!

'Let's talk in the caravan. I'll make some coffee,' he said.

Whilst Mike prepared the coffee Mereana said, 'There is only one reason they are coming home now, half way through their scholarships. Tamati has arranged this . . .'

'You don't sound very happy about it.'

'Well no . . . I'm furious! They'll be heading home because Tamati has asked them to come. He'll have told them I've left him . . . He must have booked the flights for them, because they don't have the money to do it themselves . . . I was hoping to talk to them before he made contact with them, but I've left it too long . . . and now look what's happened! It's my fault . . . I was putting it off because I didn't really know how to explain what I've done without upsetting them . . . I really should have talked to them straight after the kaumatuas came here. That would have been the right time.'

'Well, now that they know and will be home soon, you'll be able to talk to them in person. That's got to be a whole lot better than a phone call, Mereana . . . You'll be pleased to see them, even if it is all a bit unexpected. Was there any message about this from Tamati?'

'No. I just had the two text messages from the kids. Matiu's one said: 'What's going on with you and dad? Coming home immediately.' Huia said, 'Dad told me you have left him. I don't understand this. Matiu and I arrive Nelson Airport Wednesday 2.25pm.'

'Wednesday? That's tomorrow isn't it?'

'Yes. They will both be travelling as we speak. There's no way I can contact them before they arrive now . . . . and I should have been checking my phone for messages each day, but I haven't been doing it . . . not for the last few days anyway . . . I assume Huia will be meeting up with Matiu in Hawaii, or Auckland. Oh God . . . I can't think what to do for the best now . . .'

'So what do you think Tamati has in mind?'

'I can only think he may be planning to use the kids to try to get me to go back to him. I can't think of any other reason he would suddenly pull them home now. They weren't supposed to be coming back until the middle of December.'

'Maybe they are only coming for a week or so, and then going back again.'

'I hope you are right. I don't want them giving up on their scholarships halfway through. These opportunities don't come along twice! I suspect Tamati *is* just bringing them home temporarily and, if that's what he's doing, it reinforces my feeling that he wants the kids to try to do what he couldn't.'

'You'll obviously be going to meet them at the airport tomorrow, but what do you think you'll do then, Mereana?'

Mereana sat there thinking for a minute.

'It *will* be lovely to see them, but it will be awkward with Tamati there too . . . They will be very concerned about what has happened, and they'll be jetlagged, so I think I'll try to see them for a few minutes by myself. I'll try to settle things down as best I can and then arrange a time for them to come and see me over here, so we can have some time together and talk things over properly.'

'You mean you are going drive for two hours to meet them and then turn around and come back, after only half an hour or so?'

'I think I'll leave early enough to go and see Mum and Dad first. I really need to tell them what has been going on. Then I'll go to the airport and be there when the kids arrive . . . I don't want to be drawn into whatever plan Tamati has in mind, so I won't go back to our house. I want Matiu and Huia to come here, where they can see that I'm happy and where the three of us can be together without being influenced by Tamati, or anyone else. So I'll come back as soon as I've had some time with them at the airport.'

'It's good that you'll be visiting your mum and dad. I'm sure they'll want to see you . . . and they do need to hear from you . . . You realise that, if Matiu and Huia go home with Tamati, he'll have the opportunity to put his spin on everything . . .'

'I don't think there's anything I can do about that now. I've been too slow off the mark . . . He's already set some sort of agenda, so he *will* be able to put his side of the story to them first . . . He's obviously already told them enough to get them to drop everything and come all this way home. I'll just have to wait for my chance to talk to them and hope they won't have reached too many conclusions before they hear from me. I'm sure Tamati can't object to them visiting me here if I tell them I'm not going to be in Nelson . . .'

'Do you think you need to talk Tamati to find out what's going on?'

'Hmm . . . He'll be expecting me to call him I should think . . . He'll know I will have heard from the kids by now. No! I think I'll just turn up at the airport. I don't see why I should be ringing him when he hasn't had the decency to talk to me about this. No . . . I definitely think I have to show him, and the kids, that I'm doing my own thing now.'

'Fair enough! I'll have some dinner ready for you when you get back . . . and I'm going to look forward to meeting Matiu and Huia when they come over.'

Chapter 13.

Mereana decided to wait in her car, in the airport car park, until it was time for the plane to land. From her position she would be able to see the plane as it made its approach to the runway. She knew that she could then go into the terminal to have a brief word with Tamati before Matiu and Huia appeared.

When Mereana saw an ATR turboprop aircraft lining up and dropping down towards the airport she left the car and went to find Tamati. He was sitting in the arrivals area reading a newspaper when she sat down beside him.

'Tamati! Fancy seeing you here!' Mereana said with a degree of sarcasm.

Tamati ignore the bite in her tone of voice and grinned at her, looking very satisfied with himself.

'I knew you'd be here. No doubt the kids told you the flight they were on.'

'Yes. As you obviously planned it was quite a surprise to find out they were coming home all of a sudden! I'll just say that I think your way of dealing with this is pretty poor. You should have discussed it with me, before arranging anything like this. Anyhow, it's too late now, they are here. I assume they are going back again in a week or so?'

'Yes, they'll be here for ten days . . . I had to do something to keep our family together!' Tamati exclaimed belligerently.

'Tamati! Once again, you haven't been listening to me! I've already made it crystal clear that I'm not coming back to you . . . It's not going to happen! You need to accept this . . . and now the kids will have to accept it too! I'm here now because I love my kids, and of course I want to see them, but I'm heading back over to Golden Bay shortly. I just want ten minutes alone with Matiu and Huia and then I'll be on my way. I'll be telling them they have a mum and dad who both love them deeply and, even though we will not be together any more, our love and support for them will never change. I will also be asking them to come and see me in Puponga as soon as they can. In the meantime, they can go home with you . . . They'll be tired and jetlagged, so they will want to get some sleep.'

Tamati looked astonished.

'You aren't going to come home with us?'

'No! You might have planned for that to happen, but I'm not playing that game, Tamati. As I said, I just want ten minutes with them now and then for them to come to Puponga for a day or two. That's all I'm asking.'

Tamati looked quite nonplussed and was about to say something when Matiu and Huia entered the arrival area. Mereana stood up and waved. With rather anxious looks on their faces Matiu and Huia rushed over to greet their parents.

* * * * *

When Mereana got back to Puponga she drove straight to the caravan. Mike was inside preparing their evening meal. He opened the door for her and said, 'How did it go?'

'Oh, Mike . . . I feel so bad for the kids. They were so bewildered and upset. It was really, really hard leaving them to come back here. I think they felt I was abandoning them, or something, and I cried most of the way home . . . I feel like a wrung out dishcloth.'

'Come here and let me give you a hug. It must have been tough for you. How did Tamati react?'

'He was completely flummoxed when I told him I only wanted ten minutes with the kids before coming back here. That wasn't part of his plan at all. It all happened so quickly that he didn't have any time to object really. Anyhow I got my time alone with them and managed to let them know that I only found out they were coming home yesterday, when I read their texts. They were extremely surprised by that, as you can imagine! I also apologised for not telling them that I had left Tamati before they heard of it from their father and I explained that I was having trouble working out what I could say to them that would explain it all properly. They were obviously feeling hurt that they had not heard from me, but I think I calmed the troubled waters when I asked them to come and see me over here. They agreed immediately and they'll be coming for the weekend . . . as long as Tamati doesn't stop them somehow. It was so good to see them, Mike . . . They're both looking really well . . . I just hope they're not going to be too disappointed in their mum . . .'

Mereana wiped away some tears and looked quite forlorn. Mike gave her another hug.

'It sounds to me that you handled everything really well. They must be wondering why Tamati didn't tell you they were coming. I wonder what he's going to say about that! Anyway, it will be really nice for you to have them for the weekend . . . You'll have plenty of time to talk everything over.'

'Yes . . . and we'll go for some walks . . . and I want them to meet you, Mike.'

'I'm looking forward to that, but what do you think you'll tell them about me . . . us I mean?'

'If it's all right with you I'd like to tell them that we've become very good friends. It might be too early and too much of a shock for them to find out we've started to sleep together!'

'That's fine by me . . . It's early days for us anyway, isn't it . . .'

'Yes, but it would be lovely to be able to tell them we are a lot more than good friends. It's just that I don't think this is the right time . . . They have more than enough to cope with, without having to deal with their mother finding a new man so quickly!'

Mike laughed.

'Let's just do the good friends thing then. I agree that it's the best thing to do right now . . . How were your mum and dad?'

'They were obviously a bit hurt that I hadn't told them about leaving Tamati. They had heard about it from Henare and had been waiting for me to say something, so they were pleased to see me and were delighted to hear they would be able to catch up with Matiu and Huia sometime in the next few days. They were naturally concerned for me, but I was able to assure them I was fine. They wanted me to stay with them for a while, but when I said I still needed to be away from everything in Nelson they understood. I've asked them to come over here for a visit when they feel like it. I want them to meet you, Mike. No doubt they'll be hearing something about you from Matiu and Huia, so I'm sure they'll want to come over to check you out!'

'Fair enough! I'll look forward to it. Hopefully they won't put me under too much critical scrutiny. I know what parents can be like when the honour and wellbeing of their daughter is at stake!'

Mereana laughed.

'It probably won't be like that if they think we are just friends, but anyway you needn't worry . . . you would always pass the test! Now, what have you been cooking? I'm starving!'

* * * * *

On Friday morning, when she checked her cell phone for messages, Mereana learned that Matiu and Huia would be on a bus that was due to arrive at Takaka at 4.00pm that day.

'I'll pick them up and take them back to the cabin, Mike. I'm going to set up the spare beds for them. I'll cook dinner and spend the night with them . . . I hope you don't mind, but I'd like to have them with me for a while, before I introduce you . . .'

'Fine! No problem! There's no rush for them to meet me. The more time the three of you are together the better . . . You've got a lot to talk about, but you should try to have some fun too . . . You'll need to take all your things back to the cabin, Mereana. They might start to wonder about you if they see you've left your underwear and toothbrush over here!'

Mereana chuckled.

'Very true! It's going to be hard pretending we are just good friends, but it's all for the best I think.'

'I'll be discreet . . . don't worry . . . Should I offer to have you over for lunch, or something?'

'Hmm . . . Probably not, but I should ask you to have lunch with us I think. Yes! If you come for lunch tomorrow you can meet them then. I think I'll take them over to see Wharariki Beach afterwards though.'

'That's OK. I'll make my excuses after we've eaten and come back here to do some more work on the house.'

Chapter 14.

On Saturday morning Mike finished laying the last of the decking timber and started cutting newels for the deck's balustrade. At 11.30am he knocked off, had a quick shower, and changed into jeans and a warm brush cotton shirt. He was starting to feel a bit nervous about meeting Matiu and Huia. He wondered what Tamati had told them before they came and he hoped that Mereana had been able to find a good way to explain why she was now living in Puponga.

As he was lacing up his shoes he heard a knock at the caravan door.

'Mr Robinson? I'm Huia. Mum asked me to tell you that lunch is nearly ready.'

Mike knew that Huia was seventeen years old and he had expected to see someone who looked like a fresh faced schoolgirl. However, if he hadn't known otherwise, he would have guessed this very attractive young lady was at least twenty two. He could see her likeness to Mereana and realised that this was what her mother would have looked like at the same age.

'Hello, Huia! Please call me Mike . . . and thanks for coming over. I'm about ready, so I'll walk back with you.'

Huia flashed him a lovely smile and looked towards the house.

'Hey! A log cabin! Looks like it's nearly finished . . .'

'The outside is almost finished, Huia. I'll be able to take the scaffolding down soon, but there's still a lot to do inside. It's going to keep me busy for a few months yet. How are you feeling after your long flight?'

'I'm starting to get over the jetlag now, thanks. Still need to catch up on some sleep though . . . Hey! Look! There's a korimako on your harakeke over there!'

'Korimako?'

'Yes, bellbird. Mum always likes us to call the birds by their Maori name. To us the bellbird is the korimako.'

'I think I must have heard that at some stage, Huia, but I had completely forgotten . . . and I can see two of them there, in amongst the flax. They are my favourite bird around here. I love to hear them calling . . . There's such a flute-like quality to the sound they make . . . and the male bird looks quite handsome I think, with purple-coloured feathers on its head and olive green on its body. The females are a little more nondescript, though, being a more brown colour.'

'I can tell you really like them . . . I like them too! . . . The harakeke is a kind of flax. It's what we use for our weaving.'

'Well that I did know, Huia. When the harakeke is in flower there are always bellbirds and tuis around. They really like the nectar. I find them fascinating to watch . . .'

At the cabin Mereana introduced Mike to Matiu. Matiu looked at Mike quizzically as they shook hands. Mike's first impression was that Matiu looked a lot like his dad. He seemed fit and strong, but perhaps not as open or friendly as Huia had been from the start.

'I'm pleased to meet you, Matiu. Please call me Mike. Your mum has told me you have been in Hawaii lately.'

'Yes. I've been living and studying in Honolulu.'

'Are you doing some surfing too?'

'A little, but I'm not very good yet. I run mostly.'

Mereana interrupted.

'OK, people, let's come inside for some lunch.'

Lunch was a ham and cheese salad, with rocket lettuce, cherry tomatoes, French bread and fruit. As they ate Mereana told Matiu and Huia how she had been out walking nearly every day to explore the area and had loved being able to soak up all the raw beauty of the place. She recounted how she had first met Mike, when she needed help to rescue the ewe that had bogged down, and explained how they had become good friends since then, being next-door neighbours and both on their own. Matiu and Huia were clearly intrigued by her account of the old pa site and its significance as a refuge for local Maori to retreat to when they were in danger of attack by warriors from North Island and their enemies to the south. As she spoke to her children her eyes sparkled and when she looked at Mike she smiled broadly. She seemed happy and Mike wondered what Matiu and Huia would be thinking. Maybe they were seeing a side of their mother that they hadn't seen very often.

'Why don't you explain about the house you are building, Mike,' she suggested.

'All right . . . I'm trying to build an eco-friendly place. It will be self-sufficient for electricity and water and will have composting toilets. I'm determined to use as many local, natural materials as I can. I'm an engineer by training and I've always wanted to build this type of house. The main structure is built of logs, so it looks a bit rustic . . . I'm going to use solar and wind generated power and collect and recycle rain water and so on. I'd be happy to show you if you have time to come and look around . . . Your mum has given me a hand at times, when I couldn't do things on my own. I think she's an excellent builder's labourer!' Mike said with a grin.

'I'd like to have a look,' Matiu said.

'Me too!' added Huia.

'OK. Just come on over any time!'

Over lunch Mike had glanced at Mereana a few times, but he couldn't gauge how things were panning out between her and the children. They hadn't said very much and it had been up to Mereana and him to make most of the conversation. He realised that everyone was behaving very properly, trying to do and say the right thing, but there were some awkward pauses when the conversation dried up temporarily, before someone spoke again. Mike felt an air of tension, but nobody said anything about Tamati, or the separation, or why Mereana was now living in isolated Puponga. When everyone had finished eating Mereana announced that the dishes should just be put and left in the sink.

Matiu asked, 'Where did you say we are going this afternoon, Mum?'

Mike took this as a signal that it was time to take his leave.

* * * * *

The next morning Mike was busy drilling bolt holes in the newels he had cut for the balustrade when Matiu and Huia appeared.

'Good morning! How was it over at Wharariki yesterday?' Mike asked.

'Morena, Mike,' Matiu replied.

Huia smiled and said, 'Kia ora . . . Wharariki is amazing. Such a beautiful beach and the scenery there is so dramatic!'

'It's one of my favourite places,' Mike replied. 'On a good day that is . . . It's not such a good place to be if the wind is blowing hard, which it does do a bit over there. You can get yourself sand-blasted if you are on that beach in a strong wind!'

'We saw plenty of seals,' Matiu said. 'There's probably plenty of fish around there. Could be good for surf casting . . .'

'Yes! Kahawai are quite plentiful all along that part of the coast. The most popular place for surf casting seems to be Fossil Point, which is just a bit north of Wharariki.'

'If you don't mind Huia and I would like to ask you about something,' Matiu said. 'We told Mum that we were coming over to look at your house, but this is more important.'

'Oh yes? What did you want to ask?'

'We want to know what is going on with you and our mother,' Matiu said in a slightly aggressive tone and looked fixedly at Mike.

Huia glanced at Matiu with a look of disapproval, but said nothing. Mike's warning bells started to ring and he wondered what had prompted this.

'What do you mean, Matiu?' Mike asked.

'Well it's obvious that you two are not just friends. We aren't blind. We can see how you are around each other!' Matiu stated.

Huia quickly spoke up.

'We could tell by the way you both behaved at lunch yesterday that something wasn't quite right. It was like you were both holding back, or something . . . and we've talked to Mum quite a bit now and she is always mentioning you. I don't think she realises how obvious it is that something is going on between you. So we thought we'd ask you.'

Mike sighed.

'If that's what you believe, don't you think you should be asking your mum about it?'

Matiu quickly responded and said, 'You obviously know that Mum has walked out on Dad. We are still struggling to understand that and Mum is having a hard time trying to explain why she did it. Then we meet you and it's obvious something is going on. Maybe you're the reason Mum left Dad!'

Mike was taken aback, but he looked Matiu in the eye and said, 'You don't believe in holding back do you young man! OK! Here's how it is! I did not know your mother before she came to Puponga. Even then it was almost a week before we spoke. Your mum told you how we met at lunch yesterday. She wanted my help to pull a sheep out of a creek. So, clearly, I had nothing to do with the reasons your mum had for deciding to leave your father and come here. And by the way, I have met your father. He came over here with some of your kaumatuas to try to get your mum to go back to him. Those kaumatuas left here fully understanding and accepting that Mereana did not want to return to Tamati.

'As far as your mum and I are concerned I can say that I am very proud to be her friend. I am privileged to know her. She is a very fine person and you should both be very proud of her. We enjoy each other's company and we have fun together. It's true that we have become more than just good neighbours.'

'I think Mum might be falling for you, Mike,' Huia said, looking at Mike expectantly.

Mike could see that he needed to be straight with Matiu and Huia. They had obviously guessed what was happening and they needed to understand more so they could deal with it. If he was evasive, and didn't respond to their questions, they could easily leave Puponga with quite the wrong impressions of him and, more importantly, their mother. He decided to be quite open with them.

'I think I feel the same about your mum as she feels for me,' Mike said.

'How come she wants to be with you?' Matiu said rudely. 'You are old enough to be our grandfather!'

'Yes, you're right about that. You'll need to ask your mum if you want to know why she wants to be with me, but perhaps I could tell you something about the way I feel about her.'

Huia nodded approvingly and said, 'When Dad told us Mum had left him it was a real shock. We couldn't believe it! Dad said she had gone a bit crazy and wanted to totally change from the way she's always been. You can imagine how worried we were . . .'

'I *can* imagine that, but I can assure you she wasn't crazy. Your mother is a very intelligent and rational person. She doesn't suddenly do things on the spur of the moment. She thinks seriously about what she needs to do . . . and when she makes her decision she has the courage to follow through and do it. To decide to leave your dad was a huge step for her, but from what she has told me it was a decision that has been on the cards for a long time. When you both left New Zealand, to take up your scholarships, she knew that the time had arrived when she could consider what she wanted to do with her life. Up 'till then, when she was so heavily involved with her teaching, her work at the marae, and being a good mother to you two, she had felt she should not change anything. So you weren't aware she had been thinking of leaving your father for a long time. She didn't want you to have to deal with that then. But now that you are older, and you are likely to be off living your own lives from now on, she felt she could take some time to review what she wanted to do. That's why she came over here.'

'But we always thought she and Dad were happy. They did everything together and they were married for twenty years! How can you suddenly give up on that?' Matiu cried.

'Again, you need to talk to your mum about that. For what it's worth, I think your parents always did what other people expected them to do. They are both steeped in Maori culture . . . They were chosen to become leaders among your people . . . and they felt a responsibility. Part of it is that they have great respect for their elders. I think they always ended up doing what their parents and kaumatuas suggested they do . . . and that was all about working for the benefit of people in your community. I suspect they never had enough time for each other. They seem to have developed some sort of working partnership, one that your mum was prepared to maintain for the good of those around her. However, that kind of partnership arrangement was ultimately not enough for your mum. She felt she wanted more than that, and now she has taken the decision to change things and try a different pathway . . . one where she can hopefully find a greater sense of personal fulfilment than she has had before.'

'How come you know so much about it?' Matiu asked, with less aggression this time.

'I have got to know your mum very well. We talk, and we share our thoughts and feelings. We are completely open with each other. She knows a lot about me now and I like to think I understand her. We are happy in each other's company. I know this can seem rather odd, seeing I am so much older than her, but it just happened . . . It wasn't something we planned . . . When your mum came here we started out as neighbours. Then we became friends and then, well, more than friends. It was a gradual thing and I feel so lucky and honoured, because your mum is a beautiful, wonderful person!'

Huia looked troubled.

'It's been so hard for Dad. He doesn't understand why Mum left him. He feels really hurt. It doesn't seem fair that he's suddenly alone!'

Mike realised from Huia's comments that she didn't know about her father's violence towards Mereana. Obviously Mereana hadn't wanted to say anything that would reflect badly on Tamati. Fair enough . . .

'As I understand it, Huia, your dad is still heavily involved with his work for the Waimea Corporation and for the marae, *and* he is still very busy preparing the Wakatu-Mohua Claim. He won't be alone, but obviously he will be going home to an empty house at night. I guess he is finding that hard . . . I really hope he will find a way to get past all this and move on with his life.'

'He shouldn't be in this position! I still don't get why Mum walked out on him!' Matiu complained.

'She has her reasons, Matiu. You need to talk to her some more I think.'

Huia looked at Mike curiously.

'I spoke to Henare Whataroa yesterday, before we caught the bus. He said he'd met you and thinks you are a good person.'

'Did he now? I'm pleased! He struck me as being very wise and I'm sure he will continue to be a good mentor for your mum and your dad, when they need someone to talk to.'

At that point Mereana appeared. She hugged Matiu and Huia and then stood next to Mike. Seeing their expressions she said, 'What? This looks all very serious. What have I interrupted?'

Huia quickly said, 'Oh, nothing much Mum. We were just getting to know Mike a little.'

'That's nice . . . I just came to tell you two that lunch will be ready in a few minutes . . . What do you think of Mike's house?'

Looking meaningfully at Mike Matiu said, 'I think Mike was just about to give us the guided tour, Mum.'

Mereana was surprised they hadn't already looked over the house and she quickly glanced at Mike. He gave her a reassuring nod.

'Let's start with a quick look at the plans and then I'll show you how far I've got with the build,' he said.

Matiu and Huia quickly followed Mike as he made for the house, leaving Mereana standing there with a frown on her face and wondering just what she had been missing.

* * * * *

Matiu and Huia were politely complimentary about everything as they looked around the house, but Mike could tell they weren't really focussed on what they were seeing, or hearing from him. They were obviously still thinking about the conversation they had just had, before their mother had arrived.

After they left to have their lunch Mike heated up a can of soup and made some toast for himself. As he sat and ate he imagined the kind of questioning Mereana was now being subjected to and he hoped he had not said more to them than he should have. He was worried for Mereana, but there was nothing he could do but wait to hear from her later.

Before making a start on bolting the newels to the side of his deck Mike decided to take a walk out around the island and peninsular. The tide was out and after crossing the road he was able to walk straight out from the beach. He hadn't gone far when he heard the sound of someone running up behind him. As he glanced back he saw Matiu approaching.

'Hey Mike! You mind if I walk with you for a bit?' Matiu asked, as he came alongside and matched Mike's walking pace.

Feeling very surprised Mike said, 'Sure! I'd be glad of your company.'

'I have an apology to make, Mike. I was very rude to you this morning. I'm sorry . . . It seems I got things a bit wrong . . .'

'You did sound a bit angry, Matiu, but I didn't take any offence. I think I understand how you must feel about what has happened. It can't be easy to understand, or to deal with it.'

'Well, I should have listened before I made up my mind shouldn't I. It's something I have to work on. But anyway, I just wanted to say that I think you are OK. Mum likes you and she has always been a great judge of character. So, if she thinks you are a good person that goes for me too . . . And I want to thank you for helping Mum deal with all that trouble with the cannabis dealers. She told us all about it over lunch. Sounded quite nasty with them threatening her and dumping a dead sheep in the cabin! . . . She was really was grateful that you got involved and supported her . . . So am I.'

'Well thanks, Matiu. You've made my day! I wouldn't have wanted us to be at arm's length with each other . . . I happen to think you are OK too! The concern you've shown for both your parents is really good to see and, as far as the cannabis dealers are concerned, I was only too pleased to help. I'm just glad those buggers are going to be out of harm's way for a long time! Drug dealers are like cancer in my opinion . . . We definitely don't want them in our community. The harm they cause is horrendous!'

'I agree . . . I know a few people I went to school with who are really messed up now, because of cannabis and meth and stuff. They've become complete no-hopers!'

They continued walking in contemplative silence for a few minutes and then Matiu said, 'Mum also told us at lunchtime that she is very happy right now. Huia and I are still finding it hard to understand why she wasn't so happy with Dad, but she said their marriage never turned out to be what she had hoped for. It was pretty hard for us to hear that . . . because we love them both and we never had any inkling that Mum wasn't totally happy . . . It seems so sad she had to wait twenty years to do something about it.'

'Yes, but she was totally happy with you and Huia . . . Still is of course! She was also happy with her teaching and what she was doing at the marae. So it wasn't as if her life was a misery . . . far from it!'

'Yeah, well I hope she will find what she is looking for now . . .'

'So do I, Matiu . . . You and Huia seem very close . . . How do you think Huia's handling it all?'

'Better than me actually. I think she has that women's intuition. She's definitely better at the empathy thing than me. Right now she'll be telling Mum that we are both going to be able to deal with whatever happens and that we just want her to stay happy. I think we're going to take a while to fully accept she will never get back together with Dad, but that's the way it is . . . We'll have to get used to it . . .'

'Your mum will be so pleased that you are both prepared to see things this way, Matiu. I think she has been terrified that you might turn against her for walking out on your dad.'

'Not going to happen! Not now that we've come here and seen how excited she is about her future . . . whatever that's going to be.'

'Your dad will need that same kind of understanding from you both too! His life is changing as well, and he didn't see this coming!'

'Dad will be OK once he has got over what's just happened. He's pretty good at managing things. It's just that he wasn't expecting anything like this. Huia and I have a better idea of what to say to him now I think.'

Mike had been so engrossed in the conversation that he had hardly been aware that they had nearly completed the loop around the island and peninsular. He'd been vaguely aware of passing a few basking seals and a large group of oystercatchers, but his concentration had been on Matiu and he had to admit the young man impressed him greatly.

They waded across the estuary outlet and then walked back along the road. When they reached the driveway to the cabin Mike held out his hand to Matiu. As they shook hands Mike said, 'Thanks, Matiu. I enjoyed the walk and I appreciate you talking to me.'

'Kia ora, Mike,' Matiu replied.

Chapter 15.

By three o'clock Mike had the last of the newels bolted into place and he decided to make a cup of tea before starting work on the top rail. As he walked to the caravan Mereana came through the gate.

'Hi! I'm about to make a cup of tea . . . Want one?' Mike asked.

'I'd love one, Mike! I came to tell you that Matiu and Huia have asked to stay another night before going home. So, how about joining us for dinner?'

'Sounds good to me . . . I'd love to. Do you have enough food? I could zip over to Fossil Point and see if I can catch a couple of kahawai if you like.'

'That would be good. I am running a bit low on things. I have enough sausages and some vegetables, but kahawai beats sausages hands down.'

'OK. Let's have that cuppa and then I'll see what I can manage to catch.'

As they sat down to have their tea Mereana said, 'Mike, I don't know what you did with the kids earlier, but they are so much more relaxed with me now. You must have said all the right things, because when they came home for lunch their attitudes were quite changed. Instead of thinking I have been totally unreasonable and irresponsible they seemed prepared to listen to my point of view with an open mind. We had a really good talk and I think they are going to accept that I've made my choices and won't be changing my mind. They have seen how much happier I am now and it looks like they are prepared to accept whatever happens between you and I.'

'That's fantastic! I'm so glad! I'm very impressed with both of them. You and Tamati should be very proud . . . I suppose you know that Matiu and I went for a walk together. He apologised for being a bit rude earlier and he told me things were going to be all right between the three of you.'

'I'm sorry he was rude, Mike. He told me about it and was embarrassed. He said he shouldn't have jumped to conclusions and that you had made some things a lot easier to understand.'

'He didn't upset me, Mereana. I could see he was struggling to deal with what had happened . . . and he was seeing things from Tamati's point of view at that stage. Now that he's heard from you he's bound to have a more balanced understanding of things. At least he was prepared to listen and reconsider. He deserves credit for that . . . I assume you haven't said anything about Tamati hitting you?'

'No! I don't intend to . . . and I really appreciate that you haven't mentioned it either . . . The way things are going at the moment there doesn't seem any need for them to hear anything about that. We have suddenly become more relaxed around each other . . . and I really love having them here! I can see so much more maturity in them compared with six months ago. They've become more adult in their ways . . . Huia is being a real honey, Mike. She is very perceptive for her age and saw straight away that I am determined to stand my ground. She understands that I am feeling really good about having a future on my own terms . . . and she likes you too!'

'Great! I see a lot of you in her actually, but I see more of Tamiti in Matiu. As I said, I'm really impressed. They are great kids . . . I guess dinner might be a bit more angst free than yesterday's lunch was! . . . Um, I'd better get going and see if I can hook a couple of good sized kahawai.'

'I'll see you a bit later then . . . Come over when you get back, OK?'

* * * * *

This time it was Huia who chased after Mike. He'd opted to drive to the start of the Fossil Point track to save some time. He turned left out of the gate and was about to accelerate away when he saw Huia running from the cabin waving at him. He stopped and waited.

'What is it, Huia?'

'Mum said you were going to Fossil Point . . . Do you mind if I come? I'd like to see what it's like there.'

'You'll have to hang around for a while whilst I do some surfcasting, but if you don't mind that I'm very happy for you to come. Hop aboard!'

'Thanks, Mike . . . How far do we have to walk?'

'Once we get to the track it's about a thirty minute walk to Fossil Point. We'll go across the farm at the base of the spit. You'll need to look out for cow pats and sheep droppings!'

'Can I see any fossils over there?'

'Yes. I'll show you were to look and you can search for them while I'm fishing. You should be able to see fossils of ancient shell fish in some of the rocks that have fallen away from the cliff there.'

'What are you going to use for bait, Mike?'

'I've got some mackerel I caught in the estuary. Mackerel seems to be quite good bait for kahawai, but we'll have to wait and see if it does the trick today.'

* * * * *

'How was the fossil hunting, Huia?'

'Good! I found quite a few. I wasn't sure what to expect at first, but then when I finally saw one it was easy to find quite a few more . . . I see you have already got one fish.'

'Yes. It's a bit small though. I'll need to catch another one at least.'

'Mike, when we talked to you this morning you said Mum had her reasons for leaving Dad. I've been surprised at how happy she seems now . . . It's like a great weight has been lifted from her shoulders. I can't believe I never knew that she wasn't completely happy before. She always seemed to be OK, but I guess I just took things for granted. Now that I've seen her feeling really happy, despite her worries about those drug dealers, I realise that she must have done the right thing . . . Mum has tried to explain that she needs to make a change to her life and that obviously means she doesn't love Dad enough to stay with him. I can accept that now, but I don't think she has told us everything.'

Huia looked expectantly at Mike.

'Hang on a minute. I have to recast my line . . . It's being swept in by the tide.'

This gave Mike a few moments to reflect on his answer to Huia.

'You know, Huia. I think we all have things that we will never divulge to another person. There are certainly some things about me that I'm not willing to talk about . . . Sometimes these things can be hurtful to others if they come out and sometimes they can be things about ourselves that we are a bit ashamed of . . . I'm talking about deeply personal things . . . Maybe your mum has some personal things she doesn't want to talk to you and Matiu about . . . All I can say is that I'm sure she would never hold back on her love for you. I've seen the way she lights up when she's with you . . . and it's the same with Matiu . . . If I were you I'd accept things the way they are and enjoy being with your mum. You'll soon be going back to Denmark and it'll be another five months before you can see her again.'

Huia frowned and looked very thoughtful.

'I know what you are saying about keeping some personal things to yourself. I have a couple that I'd never tell a living soul . . . And I know what you mean about Mum lighting up around us . . . She lights up around you too, Mike. I know she is going to be very happy with you.'

'If I can make your mum happy I'll be the luckiest man around, Huia. I can promise you I'll be doing my best.'

'I know . . . I'm not so worried about Mum now, but I *am* really worried about Dad. He isn't at all happy at the moment. He seems really down.'

'I doubt that your dad is the type to let anything get him down for long. Once he accepts that he needs to make adjustments and deal with Mereana not being there I'm sure he will be OK . . . You know, sometimes when a change is forced upon us it all turns out for the best . . . I have a friend who suddenly lost his employment through redundancy, through no fault of his own. The company he had been with for over twenty years hit hard times, because of changes in technology. The demand for their products just started to dry up. But there he was, out of work and with a family to provide for. It was a devastating thing for him to deal with and he struggled to come to terms with it. He was quite depressed for about six weeks, but then he realised he had to make something happen . . . something positive. So he started to focus on what he should do next . . . consider all his options. What he ended up doing, actually, was to start up a small business of his own. It worked out really well and he's never looked back. He's happier now than he's ever been . . . I hope something like that happens to your dad.'

'Me too . . . but I think he's still in the depressed stage . . . Thanks for your advice, Mike.'

Mike reached out and put an arm around Huia's shoulders and gave her a reassuring squeeze. Then he suddenly jumped forward.

'Hey! I think I've got another fish! Yes! Feels like a good size! We'll be eating fish tonight, Huia!'

* * * * *

By the time Mike and Huia got back to Puponga it was almost six o'clock.

'We caught a couple of kahawai, Mereana, but I've had second thoughts about dinner . . . Seeing that it's Matiu and Huia's last night here I wondered what you would think about us all going out for dinner. It would save you having to cook . . . The fish can be put in the fridge and we could have them tomorrow. I think a meal at the Mussel Inn would be really nice. Everything is organic there: the food, the beer, and the wine. It's not fancy, but it's tasty and there's a nice rustic atmosphere about the place. What do you think? . . . It'll be my shout!'

'Wow, that's a nice idea! What do you think kids?'

'I'm up for it!' Matiu said enthusiastically.

'Me too!' Huia added.

'OK, but isn't it getting a little late now, Mike?' Mereana asked.

'I do need to have a shower and get changed, but I can be ready to leave in twenty minutes. If we leave then we can be at the Mussel Inn just before seven o'clock. It's very casual there, so we don't have to get dressed up or anything . . .'

* * * * *

Dinner at the Mussel Inn was a great success. Matiu and Huia clearly enjoyed the laid-back atmosphere of the place and the funky background music. They had never eaten in a totally organic restaurant before and were surprised at how tasty the food was. After studying the menu carefully Matiu opted for lamb and Huia decided to order greenshell mussels.

'I've been hanging out for a good meal of roast lamb for the last six months,' Matui exclaimed. 'I don't think the family I've been staying with in Hawaii know about sheep meat. The red meat is all beef over there!'

'I've been eating blue mussels in Denmark,' Huia said. 'They are tiny compared to our greenshell ones and not nearly as tasty! This is going to be so good!'

Over the meal most of the conversation was about life in Hawaii and Denmark. Matiu and Huia were encouraged to explain how they were each adapting to living with a family in a strange country, with different traditions, culture and food to their own. They were happy to compare their experiences and talk about their host families. There was a lot of laughter and it was wonderful for Mike to sit back and watch the interplay between brother and sister and mother and children. He realised there were very strong bonds between them and he could see that Mereana would never have to worry about being estranged from her children.

Towards the end of the meal Mike suggested they all drink a toast. He made sure everyone had some wine in their glass and then said, 'It seems to me that we are all at a crucial stage in our lives. I am starting out again after losing my wife. Mereana is about to enter a new phase in her life. Matiu is at university and is preparing to make his own way in the world and, in a few months time, Huia will be doing the same . . . So, I propose we drink to each other . . . and hope that whatever we do with our lives brings us joy . . . . Cheers everyone!'

The smiles showed that everyone was more than happy to drink to that and, as they raised and touched their glasses amid cries of 'To us!', Mike had a distinct sense of the goodwill flowing between them all. He felt that he was very much included in this and he suddenly experienced a wave of emotion. For a moment or two he thought of Rosie and his own children and wondered what they would make of all this. He hoped they would be pleased to know that he was happy.

Chapter 16.

After Matiu and Huia returned to Hawaii and Denmark to complete their scholarships Mereana was able to think more clearly about her future. She had heard nothing from Tamati and her relationship with Mike was deepening into something she thought could become permanent, but she couldn't stay much longer in Puponga without an income. Her funds would run out soon and she needed to start looking for a job. She resolved to discuss this with Mike as soon as they got home from the trial.

The Nelson District Court was a hive of activity when Mereana and Mike arrived at 9.30am. Sergeant Barry Sanders and the Crown Prosecutor, Gareth Williams, had arranged to meet them in the waiting area before the case was due to begin.

'We are very confident of our case, Mereana,' Gareth said. 'However, as we have already discussed, we do need to call you as a witness. I'll ask you to describe what happened after you stumbled onto the cannabis patch, and then I'll ask you to identify the three men you saw in the Ute and point out the one who followed you. I'll finish by asking you to describe what you found in your cabin later that day and to read the note they left. After I have finished you will probably be cross-examined by the lawyer who is acting for the three accused. Just stick to your story and don't let yourself be flustered in any way. Do you have any questions?'

'No. I don't think so. I just want it all to be over and for them to be sent to jail. I don't think I'd ever feel safe if they were allowed to go free for some reason.'

'I understand, but I'm sure a jail term will be imposed. Now, I'd better get going. I've just been asked to meet with Bill Edmonds, the defence lawyer, before proceedings start. Goodness knows what he wants . . . It's quite unusual.'

With that Gareth marched off. Barry showed them the door to the courtroom, but suggested they wait in the lobby until the case was called.

'I'll come out and give you a wave when you should come into the courtroom if you like. Otherwise you can go in now and see some of the other cases that are ahead of your one.'

'No. I think I'd like to wait out here if that's OK, Barry,' Mereana replied.

'All right. I'll give you a wave when you need to come in.'

'Barry obviously has some other cases as well as ours, Mereana,' Mike said. Are you feeling all right about giving your evidence?'

'I am feeling a bit nervous, but I'm also feeling determined to go through with it. I want the prosecution to succeed and for those dealers to get what they deserve.'

'Good for you! Let's sit on that bench over there.'

As they waited Mereana looked around the lobby. Quite a few people were milling about and many, like her, were obviously waiting for a case to start. Sitting opposite, a particularly tough looking character was staring fixedly at her. He suddenly leant forward and, with a nasty looking sneer on his face, pointed a finger and pretended to shoot her! Mereana was startled and she quickly looked around, but no-one seemed to have noticed. She nudged Mike who was looking at a magazine and whispered in his ear, telling him what had just happened. He quickly looked across the lobby, but the man had got up and was sauntering out the door.

'Looks like he's going, Mereana. I wouldn't worry about him. There are quite a few dodgy looking characters around and that's probably not unusual for a Court day.'

'But it seemed so personal somehow, Mike! He certainly singled me out and he was definitely giving me some kind of message. I think he might be associated with those drug people.'

'Hmm. Perhaps you are right. We'll keep an eye out for him and, if he comes back, I'll confront him.'

'What could you say, Mike? All he did was pretend to shoot me.'

'Yes, but you clearly think he was targeting you. I want to ask him what he thinks he was doing!'

Just then they saw Gareth Williams appear at the door of the courtroom and look around the lobby area. When he spotted them he scurried across.

'Good news! You won't need to give evidence after all, Mereana! There's going to be a change of plea. All three are now pleading guilty to all charges! The lawyer who was going to defend your dealers, Bill Edmonds, asked to see me to suggest they might change their plea. We've discussed the matter and it really does make sense for everyone concerned. I'm sure the weight of evidence we have against them convinced Bill that his clients were on a hiding to nothing and a full trial was going to be rather pointless. He has obviously convinced them they will serve less time if they plead guilty and avoid the trouble and expense of a trial. I'm sorry, but you've had a wasted journey today.'

Feeling very surprised Mereana said, 'Goodness. I didn't expect this! . . . But it's good . . . I'm feeling quite relieved really.'

'It certainly is good news . . . What do you think the sentence might be, Gareth?' Mike asked.

'Difficult to say . . . As you know, it's not their first offence for this kind of thing and they have made things worse for themselves by threatening to do something to do you if you reported what you saw. That's trying to pervert the course of justice and a very serious matter. So, overall, I'd expect about five years, maybe. Perhaps closer to four seeing they are going to pead guilty.'

'Does that mean they could get out in about two years with good behaviour?' Mike asked.

'Possibly not that soon . . . I'd be surprised to see them out in less than three years.'

'Doesn't seem that long to me, given their track record and the damage they are doing to so many young lives,' Mike replied.

'I agree, but we'll just have to wait to see what the Judge decides. Anyway thanks for coming.'

* * * * *

Mereana and Mike decided to have lunch at Hopgoods restaurant before they commenced their return journey to Puponga. They returned to Mereana's car to put some more money in the parking meter and then made their way to the restaurant. As they waited for their smoked salmon Panini's to arrive Mereana broached her concerns about money.

'Mike, I'm getting concerned about my financial situation. I don't have much money left and I'll have to start earning an income soon. I think I'll have to move out of Puponga and find a teaching job. The best chance of a job will be in Nelson, simply because that's where most of the schools are. I doubt if there is much chance of a job at Golden Bay High School, but I'll certainly enquire. The problem is . . . I can't bear the thought of leaving you . . . Probably we could be together at weekends, but that just wouldn't be the same! I've come to love our time together and, just as we are really getting to know each other, I am going to have to leave . . . I'm going to hate it! And I'm worried we might . . . you know . . . drift apart or something . . .'

Mereana looked at Mike anxiously and she couldn't believe he was looking at her so smugly.

'What? Why are you looking so condescending? Can't you see I'm in turmoil? I'm really upset about this!'

'Do you think I haven't been concerned about all that too, Mereana? It's been on my mind constantly . . . for the last couple of weeks at least!'

'Well why didn't you say something?'

'I've been trying to work out a solution, that's why. Some way we can stay together. I'm quite prepared to give up Puponga, if that what it takes to keep you with me . . . and maybe that is what will need to happen. It all depends on you and what you want, but I think I might have come up with something else that could work.'

'Mike, I hope you are not thinking that you will provide everything for me if I stay with you in Puponga. That wouldn't work for me. I want to have the ability to earn some money of my own and I need to have something meaningful to do with my time. I know I could help you with the house, but it will be finished in a couple of months. What could I do in Puponga then? And I haven't forgotten my promise to my kaumatuas. I still want to do something for my people . . . And you are still looking smug, Mike! What have you got on your mind? Come on . . . spit it out for goodness sake!'

Mike laughed and sat back as the waitress delivered their Panini's.

As they started to eat Mike said, 'All right! It's just an idea that I've been thinking about in the last few days. It might be quite impractical and it might not appeal to you at all.'

'What is it then?'

'Well. What would you think of the idea of me buying your friend's property and combining it with mine in order to set up a business venture that we could manage together?'

'I can't imagine what kind of business you are thinking of, Mike? What could we do with all that land?'

'How about we set up a kind of self-catering arts and educational centre, with cabins for people to stay in and a central amenities block with meeting rooms? I reckon something like that could be used by groups of artists, or writers for workshops and retreats. I'm sure I could get artists to come to Puponga. There is so much there for people to paint and I could get some art tutors to run workshops too. Maybe you could do something similar for aspiring writers. I can also imagine groups wanting to use it for yoga, or meditation, or cultural activities . . . family reunions even. What do you think? Maybe you could run some Maori language and culture workshops. If you did something like that you would definitely be doing something worthwhile for your people. There may also be potential to have tour groups use the place. There are a lot of backpackers bussing around and exploring New Zealand as they go. Perhaps they could offload in Puponga for a few days, to explore the spit and the beaches.'

'Wow! You have been doing some thinking! . . . It sounds like a great concept! Would it be something like a motel complex that would be built?'

'Not like a motel. I would like it to be more affordable for people than a motel, so it would fit somewhere between a camping ground and a motel complex I think. I have a vision of a number of small cabins scattered amongst the trees, facing out into the bay, with paths leading to a central amenities block with showers, toilets, a laundry, a large kitchen, a lounge area and a decent sized meeting-cum-class room. The people would bring and cook their own food. We would supply the pots and pans and the crockery and so on, and we could supply the bedding if required. We would have to organise someone to do the cleaning, but mostly the people who come would look after themselves. I'm thinking that you and I could each organise a series of workshops and run them at various times during the year . . . and then offer the place to other groups when we don't need it for our own purposes. If something like this was possible I'm sure there would be enough work to keep us both busy and challenged. We probably wouldn't make a fortune, but that's not a problem. A long as we can make ends meet and have a little left over I'd be happy. The main thing would be to offer somewhere for people to enjoy their activities and develop their skills. I would find it very satisfying to be able to do that.'

'It sounds like a fantastic idea, Mike, especially the Maori language and culture workshops! . . . I think Annabelle would be happy to sell if the price was reasonable. She hasn't used the place for years and she's been paying out for rates and insurance all this time . . . But I don't think I'd have any money to put up to help pay for it all. I would be totally relying on you and I don't think that would be right. I know I own half of the house Tamati and I bought in Nelson, but I don't want to ask him to move out so it can be sold. It was my decision to leave and it wouldn't be fair to expect him to move just because I'm not there anymore. I've been thinking about assigning my share of the house to Matiu and Huia, so it can remain a family home.'

'Mereana! For goodness sake don't go thinking you have to worry about money! I have enough to do this kind of thing without asking you for anything. Building the new house is costing less than a third of what I received when I sold the house in Richmond and I do have some other money invested. I don't need to provide an inheritance for my children, because they are financially successful in their own right, and I certainly cannot see any reason to have money sitting around doing nothing! . . . You know, this idea won't work without you. I wouldn't even contemplate doing it without you being intimately and fully involved. So you would have to agree to be an integral part of the whole thing. I'm talking about us being partners, Mereana . . . if you like that idea of course. If not, I'm prepared to return to Nelson to be with you and you can return to teaching, if that's what you'd prefer.'

'So you like the idea of us staying together, Mike?'

'I certainly do, if you want to keep putting up with an old codger like me!'

'I haven't found you too old so far, have I?'

Mike laughed.

'Well you've certainly been keeping me young at heart. Long may it continue I say, but that's up to you my love.'

'Are you talking long term then, Mike?' Mereana asked tentatively.

'Forever as far as I'm concerned. I'd marry you in a flash if you would have me!'

Mereana was taken aback and she wondered if Mike was really serious. From the way he was looking at her she had the feeling his last comments had not been planned and had probably just slipped out. However, it was clear that he meant what he had said. She took a deep breath and gave him a beaming smile.

'If that's your way of proposing to me, I'll accept! And I really like your idea for Puponga. Count me in!'

Mike felt a jolt of elation, but this was followed by a strong feeling of doubt and concern.

'Hang on a minute, Mereana . . . I don't think I have been very fair to you, putting you on the spot like that . . . I meant what I said about marrying you, but there's a lot involved from your point of view and I think you need to take time and think seriously before you commit to anything.'

Mereana, frowned and felt rather deflated by this.

'Don't you think I have been thinking seriously about us, Mike? I really don't need to take time for more thinking . . .'

'Yes, but I worry about what it could be like for you when I am much older . . . Everything is really great right now . . . truly marvellous as far as I'm concerned, but what about in, say, fifteen years time? I'll be seventy-eight, going on eighty and you will only be fifty-eight, going on sixty. That's still very young and, whilst I might only have a few years ahead of me at that stage, you will probably have another twenty years ahead of you! Marrying me could leave you with a long period on your own, in your older age, and I hate to think about that.'

'Mike! Do you think I haven't thought about this? I have! It is just something I will need to face when the time comes . . . For goodness sake, I am not going to give you up just because I might be a bit lonely in later life! And, who knows, I might find myself another man then, mightn't I? . . . Seriously, though, what I am looking forward to is the next twenty years with you! I'm not going to miss out on that. You have said it's what you want and I want it too! . . . I really want us to enjoy this time together as husband and wife. It will be wonderful! . . . Now, can we forget about our age difference and get back to me accepting your proposal?'

Mike looked suitably chastened and said, 'Well, if you put it like that . . .'

'Good, that's settled then!'

Mereana leaned over the table and, despite the amused looks from other diners, kissed Mike firmly and passionately on the lips.

'God, you make me feel so good, Mereana! I'm a lucky, lucky man!'

'I'm the luckiest, Mike. I feel as though I'm in an incredible dream and everything is just perfect!'

'I know what you mean about the incredible dream! We'll have to make sure it continues. Let's get back to Puponga and start putting some flesh onto the bones of our plan.'

'OK, but when we get there, and before we do anything else, I want us to make love. I want to show you how much you mean to me.'

'I think that just might be possible . . . but we have a two hour plus drive first. Come on! Let's get going!'

* * * * *

As they approached the car park they saw the flashing lights of a Police car. It seemed to be parked alongside Mereana's Honda. Then, as they got nearer, they saw why it was there. The car was totally smashed up! All the lights and windows had been smashed and there were huge dents and gashes in nearly every part of the bodywork. The tyres had also been slashed and the car was resting on the wheel rims.

'Oh my God, Mike! Look at it! My car! It's been absolutely destroyed!'

Mike approached the Police Officer who was alongside the Honda taking a note of its registration number.

'This your car, Sir?'

'Um, no. It belongs to my partner here.'

'I'm sorry, Madam, but I'd say your car is a write-off. We got a call to say two men were attacking it with a sledgehammer and an axe! Apparently they only took about thirty seconds to do all this damage. Then they ran off and disappeared. We were told they were wearing gloves and hoodies and, unfortunately, no-one was game enough to follow them to see where they went, or try to get a registration number from their car. No-one has been able to give us a good description of the men . . . at least not so far. All we know is that they looked big and tough. That description's not much use to us I'm afraid . . . Do you know why you might have been targeted by these guys?'

Mereana said, 'I think this is a revenge attack. I was due to give evidence against three drug dealers this morning, but just before the trial started they decided to change their plea to guilty. So I didn't have to give my evidence after all, but there was this guy outside the courtroom . . . He was looking at me in a threatening kind of way and he pretended to shoot me. He was definitely trying to give me a message. I reckon he was part of this. He must have followed us back to the car when we came to top up the parking meter.'

'I see . . . You'd better come along to the Station and make a statement about all this . . . and we'll need a description of the man you think was being threatening. I can take you there in the patrol car. I see the tow truck is just arriving. It will take your car to our yard. We'll have some forensics done there, but I have to tell you I'm not confident we'll get whoever is responsible. Even if we could identify the man you saw this morning we may have no way of tying him to all this damage.'

Mereana looked at Mike in some despair.

'I know, love,' Mike said. 'Just when we thought everything was great this has to happen. Those bloody drug dealers must have arranged this. Just as well they are going to be locked up! Look . . . you go and make your statement and I'll see about getting another car, so we can go home. Let's meet back at Hopgoods when you're finished at the Police Station. If I'm not there just have a coffee or something. I shouldn't be too long.'

* * * * *

Mereana was sipping a Cappuccino when Mike arrived back at Hopgoods.

'How'd you get on with the Police?' he asked.

'Well I gave them my statement and a description of the man at the courtroom. They gave me some mug shots of local criminals, but none of them was the guy I saw this morning. However, there was a Sergeant there who thought my description could fit Kenny McCann. You remember, he was the one Barry Sanders said was the number one dealer in the region! That possibility really puts the wind up me, Mike! Anyway, they told me not to build up my hopes of them catching the culprits, but they promised to do their best. They let me clear out all my things from the car. Everything's in this bag under the table . . . Do you think this will be the end of it all, Mike?'

Mike thought for a moment.

'I would think so. They have certainly been vindictive, but I think they've probably made their point. I think everything will die down now that they are going to prison . . . I can't see the bastards who smashed up your car, or this McCann chap, wanting to take any further risk of falling foul of the Police.'

God! I hope you're right . . . What am I going to do about the car, Mike?'

'Ring your insurance company and tell them it's probably a write-off. They'll send their assessor to look at it in the Police yard. I would be very surprised if you'll ever see it again. It looked like there was far too much damage to warrant repairs, so I'd say it will be condemned. In due course the insurance company will give you whatever their assessor thinks is a fair market value. In the meantime, come with me, I've got something to show you.'

They walked just around the corner and Mike pointed to a gleaming new Kia Sportage.

'There you go . . . There's our engagement present . . .'

'Mike! Whatever have you done! You shouldn't have gone and bought a new car!'

'Why ever not? I've always liked the look of this model and we are going to need two vehicles. I think it's a lovely way of celebrating our engagement! How about you get in and drive me home? I haven't forgotten that you want to have your way with me, you know . . . .'

Mereana hugged Mike so tightly he thought he was going to stop breathing.

'Thank you so much, Mike! You are such a honey! I can't believe you just went and did that! Come on then. Let's get going so I can express my undying gratitude . . .'

'Hey! I like the sound of that!'

CHAPTER 17.

Bad weather had set in during the days following the trial and Mereana and Mike decided to delay resuming work on the new house. Mereana wanted to do some writing and Mike was keen to finish his portrait before he started preparing plans for the arts and education centre. Mereana was happy to do her writing in the cabin, but Mike had set up his easel in one of the bedrooms in the new house. They were both quite coy about the work they were doing, each wanting to make a little more progress before revealing their creations to each other.

After two days of painting, the first time Mike had used his water colours in weeks, his portrait of Mereana was nearing completion. He only needed to add some final touches of colour to the background seascape to finish it off. He was very pleased with his efforts. He thought he had managed to capture Mereana's beauty and a typical expression of hers; the one when she focussed all her attention on something and her eyes seemed to glow.

At dinner time he walked next door to the cabin and found Mereana still deeply engrossed in her writing, surrounded by reference books. She looked up in surprise as he came in and leant over her to kiss her on the cheek.

'Hello my darling. How's it going?'

'It's coming along I suppose,' Mereana replied. 'Goodness! I had no idea it was so late. You must be getting hungry.'

'I'm in no rush to eat. Why don't you finish what you were doing whilst I cook something for us?'

'No. I think I'll stop now. I couldn't concentrate with you bustling around . . . and I think it's my turn to cook anyway.'

'I don't mind . . . really! But if you prefer to cook I won't put up much of a fight. I have to concede that your cooking skills are way more imaginative and superior to mine.'

'Flattery will definitely work on this occasion, Mike! All right . . . Just let me clear away these papers and books and I'll get started.'

'How about letting me read what you have written?' Mike suggested hopefully.

'No way! I'm not quite ready for that . . . but I'm not too far off finishing the opening part of the book. When I am satisfied that what I have done is decently written I'll let you see it and you can tell me what you think.'

'OK, but how about telling me what the storyline is? I'm dying to know!'

'Let's do a deal then. I'll tell you what my book is going to be about if you show me what you have been painting.'

Mike laughed.

'I fell into that didn't I! Fair enough! It's a deal. But you first . . . You can tell me what you're doing whilst you get dinner ready and then I'll go and get my painting. How 'bout that?'

* * * * *

'I'm trying to write a historical novel, Mike. It's going to be loosely based on the history of this area . . . the area north of Takaka, including Collingwood, Pakawau, Puponga, the spit, Westhaven Inlet and Wharariki. In the old days the Maori called this land Te Tai Tapu and Golden Bay was called Mohua.

'The Tumatakokiri were the first tribe to settle in the area. They were called Tumatakokiri after a chief of that name. He was the son of Whatonga, who arrived in New Zealand from Hawaiki, wherever that was, on the famous migration canoe Kurahaupo. I'm sure you have heard that Hawaiki was the legendary starting place for all the major migration voyages to New Zealand. Hawaiki just means 'the homeland,' so it seems very likely that canoes started out from various places around the Pacific at different times. Easter Island is thought to have been the starting place for some very early migration voyages and, subsequent to that, Tahiti is thought to have been another starting-off place . . . but it is all very unclear as there are no records. Maori didn't have a written language at that time. Anyway, from the oral history passed down through the generations, we know there was definitely a lot of movement from one Pacific island to another . . . and back again sometimes. The voyagers knew how to navigate by the stars.

'Chief Tumatakokiri probably died in central North Island, in the Taupo area, but his tribe eventually migrated south from that region, via the Whanganui River, and across to the South Island. Initially they went to the Marlborough district, but they were driven westwards by the tribes there. They ended up here and remained for about two hundred years.

'When Abel Tasman first discovered Mohua he had a run-in with the Maori living near Takaka and four of his crew were killed, so he decided that Mohua should be called Murderer's Bay. That was in 1642, way before Captain Cook came along. It's called Golden Bay now, because gold was discovered here, not because of the golden sand as many people think. Anyway, there were Maori settlements all around here before the Europeans arrived. In fact Abel Tasman first realised that New Zealand was inhabited when he saw smoke rising from the pa here in Puponga!'

'Wow! I didn't realise that Tasman had seen smoke coming from right here!'

'He did, but he didn't stop here. He carried on further into the bay and that was where he made his only contact with Maori in this country, the Tumatakokiri. It was somewhere near Tata Beach. There was a huge misunderstanding, a clash of cultures if you like, between Tasman's crew and the local Maori. One theory is that the Tumatakokiri thought the Dutch were ghosts. They had never seen Europeans, or large sailing ships before. They went out in canoes and sounded their horns as a way of repelling them. However, when the Dutch sounded their trumpets in reply this was interpreted as a challenge accepted and a warlike response, rather than a return of greeting as the Dutch intended. The Dutch tried to encourage the Maori to board their ships, but neither side could understand each other and, if the Tumatakokiri thought they were being confronted by ghosts, they certainly wouldn't have been tempted to leave the safety of their canoes. Another theory is that the Tumatakokiri thought Tasman was after their food stocks. They had gardens and food storage pits in the area and it seemed that Tasman was heading straight for the spot where the food was held. The Tumatakokiri had had plenty of trouble from other tribes and they may have thought they needed to repel another attempt to steal what was theirs. So you can take your pick of what might have been the case.

'Tasman's two ships, the Heemskerck and the Zeehaen, stayed at anchor and the crew remained on board overnight. The next day the Tumatakokiri went out in their canoes again and did a haka, challenging the 'ghosts' . . . or the raiders. It was soon after that when sailors in one of Tasman's small boats were attacked as they tried to travel between the Heemskerck and the Zeehaen. Three were killed instantly and one was mortally wounded. The Dutch then weighed anchor to leave and they fired on the canoes, probably killing at least one Maori. The canoes all made a hasty retreat to shore then and Tasman sailed away. He eventually left New Zealand without ever having set foot on it.'

'I've heard about some of that before, Mereana, but I didn't know about the ghost theory, or that they might have thought their food stocks were threatened. I guess if that incident hadn't happened it is possible that New Zealand could have become a Dutch colony.'

'I don't know about that, Mike. Anyway, Tasman's visit was in 1642 and my book is set in the 1800's, so I'm writing about a much later time.'

'What happened to the Tumatakokiri people?'

'They were attacked in the 1770's by the Ngati Apa who lived on the west coast of the North Island, mainly in the Rangitikei, Manawatu and Kapiti districts. They sailed across in their canoes and caused great havoc. Then, when the Tumatakokiri tried to fight back, by mounting an attack on the Ngati Apa back in Kapiti, they suffered a major defeat . . . and of course Ngai Tahu were also attacking them from the south. The tribe was basically finished then. The survivors were taken over and absorbed into the conquering tribes . . . as slaves mostly. So Ngati Apa then became established here, but in the early 1800's the Ngati Apa were themselves defeated! This time it was Ngatiawa, under a chief named Te Koihua, who took over. Te Koihua, who was an ally of the famous Chief Te Rauparaha, ended up staying in this area. He lived just down the road near Pakawau.'

'Do you know what caused all this fighting, Mereana?'

'There could have been a number of reasons, but tribes often mounted raids to acquire more slaves, or to take revenge for some previous incident, or because another tribe had something they wanted. This area was a kind of staging post for northern Maori wanting to travel down to the West Coast to obtain greenstone, which was greatly prized and sought after. As you know, it was used in weapons and for adornment. Whoever controlled this region could control much of the greenstone supply to the North Island. The area was also very good for fishing and for shellfish, plus the regular whale strandings on the spit provided food and bone for carving. I imagine the birdlife was prolific then too, so that would have been another good source of food.'

'You have some ancestral connection to this region yourself don't you?'

'I do. My whakapapa is a mix of Ngatiawa on my father's side and Ngai Tahu on my mother's. So I have a real connection with this area.'

'My goodness! You have a warlike past, Mereana! I'll have to be on my guard!'

'Have no fear, Mike. It was always the men who wanted to fight. We women have always had to suffer the consequences of that . . . and none more so than the main character of my book, a young woman called Meri, who was the daughter of a chief of the Ngati Apa.'

'Did she become a slave?'

'Not exactly . . . Meri is a figment of my imagination, Mike, and in my book she is forced to become the wife of a fictitious son of Te Koihua, whom I have called Tama. Tama is very taken with Meri and, rather than treat her as a slave, he persuades his father to let him take her as a wife.'

'That might have been a bit like slavery anyway, if she wasn't too keen on the young man,' Mike suggested.

'Being treated as a wife would have been less debilitating physically, but probably more debilitating psychologically, especially as she would have been forced to live as wife to a man who had been instrumental in killing, or enslaving her own family . . . I am trying to describe how she comes to terms with this and how she eventually accepts her husband, makes the most of the fact that she is still alive, and has a future and children to look forward to. I'm also going to deal with the arrival of the missionaries and first British settlers, and how that impacted so badly on the Maori community.'

'I assume they lost their lands, Mereana?'

'Yes. In 1852 Te Koihua was persuaded to sell all the land north of the Aorere River for a paltry £550. He was granted a small reserve area near Pakawau, but otherwise all the area around here was transferred to the colonialists. Mathew Richmond, who was the Superintendent of Nelson, was the man who did the deal. He and the British authorities knew full well that the area had valuable coal and other mineral resources, but he was only authorised to pay a price based on the area's grazing value. Basically, Te Koihua was conned. I doubt he had any real idea of the true value of £550. It really was a pittance. Maybe he was tempted because he could use the money to buy weapons and other goods . . . but the end result was that very few Maori could continue to live here . . . and those who did had to work for the settlers for subsistence wages. The first farmer to set up here was a Scot called James Mackay. He started to run sheep and cattle in 1853 . . . and, as you know, a lot of coal was mined in Puponga during the early 1900's. Gold was also discovered and extracted from various locations around the area too.'

'Gold is still being mined in the Aorere Valley, Mereana . . . I think your novel has a very interesting plot and, with your whakapapa, you are just the right person to write about lives of Maori who used to live in these parts. I think you have all the ingredients for a fascinating story. I'm really going to enjoy reading it when you are ready.'

'I hope so, Mike . . . Now . . . your part of our bargain was to show me your painting!'

'Mmm. I'll have to go and get it then . . . I hope you aren't too shocked . . .'

Mereana looked a little baffled as Mike left the cabin. What could possibly be in a landscape painting that would shock her?

* * * * *

Mike insisted that Mereana close her eyes as he set up the painting next to the dining table.

'OK, Mereana, you can look now.'

For a few moments Mereana didn't say anything. She stood in front of the painting motionless and just looked. Then she turned to Mike and, with tears in her eyes, said, 'Mike, it's beautiful! How on earth did you do it? I haven't sat for you and you haven't taken any photos. It's amazing! I can't believe you have produced something so real . . . and you've made me look wonderful!'

'You *are* wonderful! That is just how I see you. You are beautiful . . .'

'Oh Mike, I feel so . . . honoured I suppose. I never guessed you were doing a portrait of me . . . I thought you were doing one of your landscapes . . . perhaps with some birds in the foreground or something. What possessed you to paint me?'

'When I started it I had only just met you, Mereana. I couldn't get you out of my mind. It was something I felt right about doing . . . I think I needed to . . . but I'm sorry I didn't ask your permission . . .'

'I don't really know what to say . . . I'm overwhelmed! . . . I absolutely love it, Mike. You really have great talent . . . But it isn't something we can hang in our lounge is it!'

'Maybe not, but I'm certainly not going to be selling it. I have a few finishes touches to make and then I'll have it nicely framed . . . Perhaps I should hang it in my studio?'

'Yes, that's the right place! . . . Thank you, Mike. I'll always treasure it. It's such a lovely surprise. It makes me feel kind of special.'

'Well that's all right then,' Mike said with a grin. 'I certainly got a lot of pleasure doing it. Come and give me a kiss, and then we should eat . . .'

CHAPTER 18.

Ten days after their trip to Nelson Mike received a letter from Julia. It had been preying on his mind for the last twenty-four hours, since he first opened it, and he had suffered a very poor night's sleep as he constantly thought about what Julia had written. Now, having read the letter once again, he decided to write a reply, rather than telephone.

Mereana was at the kitchen sink, washing the breakfast dishes, when Mike sat down at the dining table to write. He was now living more or less full-time in Mereana's cabin, where there was more room, and it was nice to be able to sit in front of a log fire and use a decent-sized bathroom.

'Leave the dishes for me to dry, Mereana. I want to write this letter first though. It's a reply to a letter I got from Julia yesterday.'

'You've been pre-occupied ever since that letter came, Mike. I hope it's not bad news?'

'No. It's not bad news, but you can see for yourself. I'll show you my reply too.'

'OK . . . I'm going to hang out the washing now. Looks like we might get some rain later, so I need to get cracking.'

* * * * *

Mereana was tidying the bedroom when Mike finished his letter.

'Here you are, love. Have a look at Julia's letter first and then tell me what you think of my reply.'

'You sure you want me reading this, Mike? Julia might not want me to read her letters.'

'Well it concerns you, Mereana, and I have no doubt you should see it.'

'Hmm, that sounds a bit ominous . . . OK, if you're sure . . .'

'I'm sure. Go ahead.'

Dear Dad,

I hope you don't get upset with me once you have read this letter, but what I want to write is, shall we say, sensitive, and I want to ensure I express myself properly. I have found that I can usually marshal my thoughts better when I have to go through the discipline of considering how to record them in writing.

What I want to say concerns your last phone call, when you told me that you have decided to live with the lady who you have met recently, Mereana, and that you intend to marry her. I know you rang Paul to give him this news also. We have talked about your news and you should know that Paul supports what I am going to say.

First of all, our first wish is that you are, and remain, happy! When Paul and I came home for Mum's funeral we were all so full of sadness and grief that I don't think any of us could look into the future and see what lay ahead for you. Obviously we knew you would be alone and lonely without Mum. We know how much you loved her and it must have been so hard for you to come to terms with her sudden loss. Unfortunately, after Mum's funeral, Paul and I had to return to Jenny and Peter and the kids, and to our jobs in London. You said you wouldn't come with us at that time and we understood you had all sorts of things to attend to, but we did feel awful about leaving you then.

It has been really good to keep in touch through our regular phone calls, but they will never substitute for talking face to face will they? You have always told us that you are managing well and getting on with life and, when you said you had sold the house and were building in Puponga, we realised that you were leaving painful memories behind and trying to make a fresh start. Paul and I talk about you quite often and we both feel that giving yourself a project to build a house in Puponga is a very good way of making a transition to the next part of your life. But, to be honest, we only ever saw your move to Puponga as a temporary thing. It's such a small place and we worry that there isn't enough opportunity for social interaction. We don't like the idea of you remaining isolated way out there, without your friends and all the usual things around you that living in a reasonable sized community can offer.

When you told us about Mereana it was obvious that you were excited to have someone to be with. But when you told us she is recently estranged from her husband we naturally worried that you were both being drawn together for the wrong reasons. She has left her husband and you have lost your wife, so you are both bound to be lonely and in some kind of emotional turmoil. Probably you are both finding it difficult to contemplate the future and see a way forward. We can understand that being thrown together in Puponga in such circumstances could provide the opportunity for each of you to overcome, at least to some extent, the significant gap in your lives caused by no longer having your partners. To be perfectly frank, Paul and I wonder if you have been too quick to decide that you want to enter into another relationship and to be thinking of getting married so soon.

Please know that we don't have any judgement to make about Mereana. We don't know her, or anything about her, except that she has left her husband and her teaching job and, until now at least, has been very active in Nelson's Maori community. Knowing you as we do we are totally confident that Mereana will be a lovely person—you have always been an excellent judge of character, Dad. But your relationship with her seems to have developed from neighbourly friendship to the point that you are now talking about marriage so rapidly! I hope you can understand why we feel a little concerned about that, especially when you are both living away from everything you have been used to and when you are trying to come to terms with the momentous things that have happened in your lives.

Dad, please don't think we wish to interfere in your personal business. Our concerns come out of love for you and we just want you to have the best possible life and always be happy. Naturally you will make your own decisions, and you have always been an excellent decision-maker, but please could you consider what we are saying? Even better, how about coming to London to stay with us for a while? If you can come quite soon we could discuss all this in a more relaxed and appropriate way. It is very difficult trying to discuss such sensitive and personal matters without seeing you face to face. Paul and I would love to see you and of course Jenny, Peter, Jesse, Daniel and Connor need to see you too! The kids are developing so fast and we don't want you to miss too much of their early years.

It has been great to hear about how well you are getting on building your log house. You must be justifiably proud of your efforts.

Please ring and let us know if you can come to London. In the meantime, please give our best wishes to Mereana. We would love to see some photos of her.

All my love
Julia (and Paul)
PS—How about sending us some photos of the log cabin too?

As Mereana read Julia's letter she paused a couple of times to look thoughtfully across at Mike, but he was carefully avoiding her gaze. When she finished it she said, 'Your kids really care about you, Mike. You must be proud of them. I can understand exactly what they are worried about and why they want you to go to London. I'd totally understand if you want to go . . . Maybe it would be for the best . . .'

'Let's talk about it after you have seen my reply. OK?'

With that Mike left the bedroom and Mereana felt distinctly uneasy as she picked up Mike's letter.

Dear Julia and Paul,

I received your letter yesterday and have spent some hours thinking about it.

First of all I want to thank you taking the trouble to tell me about your concerns, and I do realise that they are genuinely felt and well meant. So please don't worry that you might have upset me in any way—I'm not upset! I just feel privileged that you feel able to raise these things with me, and have them out in the open, so we can deal with them. The love we share as a family is obviously strong enough that we can say what we think without feeling we are going to alienate each other, or cause too much upset.

Secondly, thank you for inviting me to visit you in London. I think this is a good idea, but more about that later.

The points you made in your letter are, of course, things I have considered over and over again myself, when I realised that my relationship with Mereana was developing into something much more than basic friendship. However, you can be assured that I am not rushing my fences and acting precipitously. It is true that we have come a long way in a short time together, but I am confident that our feelings for each other are genuine and lasting. I can see how anyone could think that we been drawn to each other because of our personal circumstances, especially the fact that we both find ourselves without our partners after many years, and that we should be cautious about committing to any long term relationships for this reason. What actually happened was that we immediately felt at ease in each other's company and we found that we had a special bond right from the start. I don't think this was anything to do with our new status as 'singles'. Neither of us had any intention of seeking out someone to fill any kind of gap in our lives. We just happened to meet and we hit it off. This has been quite incredible for me as I had thought that, at my age, I was destined to be on my own from now on, and I was quite resolved and happy to remain that way. When Mereana came along I initially thought we would be good friends and neighbours, but quite unexpectedly things developed beyond that and we found ourselves wanting to be together all the time. Like me, Mereana had no intention of entering into any new relationship. She was trying to deal with the end of her marriage and another partner, or husband was the last thing on her mind.

What we find is that we have a genuine desire to share everything and live our lives together. We make each other very happy and we have plans for this to continue. We both love Puponga and we are hoping to remain and develop a business here. We both accept that Puponga is a tiny place and rather isolated, but we like it, and we can always take a drive to Takaka, or Nelson if we want to take advantage of the facilities and communities there, or visit friends.

I want you both to know that I always loved your mother deeply. I still think of her every day with great affection and I feel her loss. She will always be in my heart. Much to my great surprise I have now found I can love someone else as well and achieve something like the same happiness I had with Rosie. But this is a different kind of relationship, because Mereana is a different person. She isn't like Rosie and never will be. She is, never-the-less, another wonderful person. I have grown to respect and admire her tremendously. Mereana will never replace, or be a substitute for your mum and she wouldn't even want to try to be like this. She has children of her own and, likewise, she realises that I could never replace, or substitute for their father. He of course will remain in their lives and I will encourage this. I have met Matiu and Huia and I was very impressed with them. They are developing into fine young adults and they think the world of both their parents. It has been hard for them to understand why their mum and dad are no longer together, but they have accepted the situation. I think Matiu, Huia and I will be friends. Having seen how happy Mereana is *here, and with me, they told me that they have no problem with our relationship. This meant a great deal to me and of course Mereana was mightily relieved too.*

So, I hope you understand that Mereana and I are not rushing blindly into a relationship to compensate for what we have lost. We are not trying to recreate our past somehow. Instead, and quite unexpectedly, we have a chance of a new kind of happiness and we intend to make the most of it.

I'd like to come to see you in London quite soon, but I would want Mereana to come with me. If she agrees I'll book flights and accommodation (I don't want you to feel you have to put us up. I know how busy you are with the kids and your jobs). Just let me know if you are planning to be away from London for any periods of time in the next month or two, so I can make sure our arrangements fit in with yours. I want Mereana to meet and get to know you both. I want her to see why I am so proud of you and for you to see why it is that we are so happy together.

Please give Jesse, Daniel and Connor a big hug from me and tell them I hope to see them again soon.

Much love
Dad

Mike was sitting at the dining table, nervously waiting for Mereana's response to the letters, when she emerged from the bedroom.

'Wow, Mike! What can I say? Are you the most perfect man in the world, or what! Your letter made me cry! What you said was wonderful . . . I can't think of anything I'd change or add . . . and I feel exactly the way you do! I know everything has been happening so fast for us, but I'm not at all worried about that. We have enough experience of life to be aware of what we are getting into. There was no way I was looking for another relationship, but like you said it just happened, and I'm as surprised as you are about it. But it really does feel like it was meant to be and I wouldn't change a thing!'

'It does feel right, but how do you think Julia and Paul will react to my letter, Mereana?'

'It may not allay all their fears, but it tells them you are quite sure about what you are doing. Probably they will remain concerned until they see you and I think the idea of us both going to London is fabulous! They need to see that I'm not some kind of desperate woman, or a gold-digger or something! I feel so blessed that you are so thoughtful and caring . . . I'll be as nervous as kitten when I meet Julia and Paul, but they will have to get to know me at some time won't they! I hope that, in time, they will let me feel part of your family. If we go we could probably arrange to go to see Huia in Copenhagen and include Hawaii in the itinerary as well, so we can see Matiu too. A trip like that would be wonderful! I've never travelled further that Sydney before, so it will be an adventure too! I'm really excited!'

Mike smiled happily and he stood up and opened his arms. Mereana stepped into his embrace and they hugged each other excitedly.

'I'm so glad you approve of everything, Mereana,' he whispered. 'And of course we'll go and see Huia and Matiu as well. That's a great idea and I should have thought of it!'

They were still in each other's arms when a car drove up to the cabin.

'Oh my God! It's Mum and Dad!' Mereana cried.

When Mereana quickly looked around the room she saw that it would be obvious to her parents that she and Mike were living together. She looked at Mike despairingly and he immediately understood why she looked so panicked.

'Don't worry,' he said. 'There's nothing we can do about it. They have to know how things are between us sooner or later . . . It may as well be now. Let's go out and meet them . . .'

'Mum! Dad! What a great surprise! It's lovely to see you!'

'We thought we'd surprise you, Mereana, but it was us that got the surprise when we drove in and saw you two through the window!' Jenny Parata exclaimed.

George Parata grinned wryly and said, 'I told you we should have rung first!'

They both gave Mereana a hug and then turned to Mike.

'Good morning! You must be Mike. We've heard something about you from our grandchildren. Please call me Jenny . . . and this is my husband, George.'

As Mike shook their hands he said, 'I'm really pleased to meet you!'

'You'd better come inside so we can tell you our news,' Mereana said.

Jenny and George quickly looked at each other and moved towards the cabin. Inside Mereana suggested they all sit around the dining room table.

'Can I get you a cup of tea, Mum? How about you, Dad?'

'Tea would be good, Mereana,' Jenny replied.

'I'll have coffee if that's all right,' George said. 'But you'd better tell us what this news is. You've got us wondering . . .'

Mereana looked quickly at Mike and saw him nod reassuringly.

'Well . . . no doubt you heard from Matiu and Huia after their visit here. I'm sure they told you something about Mike and how we have been seeing each other?'

'Yes,' Jenny replied. 'They said the pair of you were getting into a relationship!'

Mereana nodded.

'They were right about that. They saw it straight away . . . that Mike and I were really happy together . . . Anyway, things have moved on since then and we have started to live together. We love each other and we want to be married one day.'

George wrinkled his brow and looked at Jenny. She was looking more than a little flabbergasted.

'You haven't wasted any time then, Mereana!' he said. 'One minute we hear that you've left Tamati and, the next we hear that you've found a new man. *Now* you tell us you've moved in together and have decided to marry him!'

Mereana could see the concern on both her parents faces.

'I know it must seem like it's all happing in a rush, but that's not the way I feel about it. Mike and I are just going along with what feels right for us. We certainly found out very quickly that we love each other and we have acknowledged that by making a commitment to be married, but there's no rush to have a wedding ceremony. We haven't even talked about when that might happen and, of course, I'll have to be divorced first!'

'Goodness, I don't know what to think!' Jenny muttered. 'We weren't expecting to hear this. When did you decide all this?'

'Mike moved in with me about a week ago and we decided about getting married a few days ago. We are really happy you know!' Mereana said a little desperately.

Mike thought it was time he said something.

'Can I say something? . . . I can see how all this might look from the outside. Things *have* been happening quite fast, but that doesn't mean we are being reckless. We aren't young and inexperienced. We have considered the issues. What we are doing is right for us. I love your daughter very much and I will always put her happiness and wellbeing ahead of anything. You don't know much about me and I can therefore understand your reservations. I'll be happy to answer all your questions . . .'

'We do want to get to know you, Mike, but we should probably hear from Mereana first. I don't know about George, but I want to hear what she has to say about you!' Jenny said.

'That's fine with me, Jenny. Maybe I'll pop next door for a while and do some work on the house until you are ready to talk to me . . . But perhaps Mereana should tell you our other news first.'

Mike looked questioningly at Mereana.

She sighed and said, 'I may as well tell you the rest and get it all on the table.'

When Mereana had finished explaining about their plans to set up the arts and educational centre and to make a visit to London and Copenhagen, with a stopover in Honolulu en route, Jenny and George looked rather shell-shocked.

'I think you need to make my coffee a strong one, Mereana! I feel as though so much is happening! Phew! You sure know how to take the wind out of our sails!' George exclaimed.

'Sorry, Dad . . . I don't know how else we could've done this. A lot has been happening and most of it just in the last few days. We only decided about going to London this morning! That was why I was hugging Mike when you drove in. I was so excited! You are the first ones we have told about our plans to develop this place and Mike's two children in London are the only ones who know about our intention to get married one day . . . And they only know before you because Mike has a regular phone call with them every Sunday evening . . .'

'Well at least *we* know now, but there's such a lot to think about.' Jenny said. 'When are you planning on telling the rest of the whanau?'

* * * * *

Nearly two hours had passed and Mike was getting really worried about what was going on between Mereana and her parents. He could hardly think about what he was doing and had to keep re-measuring things as he prepared to erect the framing for a wall between the two bedrooms. Eventually, though, he heard Mereana call out and he put his tools down and went outside.

A quick look at Mereana reassured him. She was looking relieved and gave him a beaming smile.

'So this is the log house Matiu and Huia talked about,' said George as he looked up. 'It's bigger and more impressive than I imagined . . . Sorry we've been so long, Mike. We had a lot to talk about as you can probably imagine, but you don't have to worry. Mereana has sung your praises and we can see how happy she is.'

'Yes, we are starting to come to terms with everything now, Mike,' Jenny added. 'We have put Mereana through a fair old grilling and we feel a lot less anxious than we were when we first arrived.'

'I'm so relieved!' Mike said. 'I was starting to wonder whether I needed to come over and rescue her!'

George chuckled.

'She didn't need rescuing, Mike. She can take care of herself . . . She's a Parata . . . and we've always been able to look after ourselves!'

'I'll take that as fair warning then, George!' Mike said with a grin.

'Mike, I've suggested Mum and Dad stay on for a while. I don't think they should have to drive home straight away.'

'Good idea!' Mike said and then turned to Jenny and George.

'You can use my caravan if you would like to stay over tonight. It's reasonably comfortable. It would be nice to have dinner together and be able to talk . . .'

Jenny looked pleased and said, 'Why don't we stay the night, George? There's nothing that needs to be done back home that couldn't wait another day . . .'

'Fine by me,' George said. 'I'm in no hurry to get back, but I'll have to borrow a toothbrush!' he said laughingly.

Mereana said, 'That's settled then, but you men will have to catch some fish for dinner!'

'Sounds good to me, Mereana,' George responded. 'I suppose Mike already knows the best spots around here . . . If there's time, though, I'd like to have a look at your new house . . . and also go on to the old pa site.'

'It shouldn't take too long to catch a fish or two. We can certainly do all that, George,' Mike said. 'I've got a spare surf caster. So, between the two of us, I'm sure we'll hook some kahawai.'

'Looks like the men are all sorted, Mum. What about you and me?'

'Oh, I think we'll be able to find some things to do and talk about,' Jenny said meaningfully. 'But I want to see the house too!'

'I can show it to you, Mum,' Mereana said feeling very pleased with the way things were working out.

* * * * *

With Jenny and George safely ensconced in the caravan Mereana and Mike prepared for bed.

'That was quite a day, Mereana!'

'You can say that again! But it turned out to be a lovely day!'

'Your folks seem to be coming on board with everything don't they? I thought they must have been giving you quite a hard time when they had you pinned down for just over two hours! I really *was* about to come to the rescue you know . . .'

'It was fine once I started telling them about us and all our plans. They had already heard good things about you from our kaumatuas, and from Matiu and Huia, so I think they were always going to give you the benefit of the doubt. They weren't so sure about me though. I think they were quite worried I had lost the plot! Anyhow, they gradually became more at ease with everything. They thought it was a really good idea for me to meet Julia and Paul in London and then see Huia and Matiu as well . . . and they fell in love with your idea for the centre here, especially the opportunity for me to run Maori language and culture workshops.'

'Well the whole centre thing is still just an idea. We did tell them that. We have to acquire the land and draw up detailed plans, and then we need to apply for consents to operate that kind of venture and for all the building work involved. All we have at the moment is a concept.'

'I know, but they can already see it all happening, Mike. So can I . . . I really want to do it.'

'Once we find out if we can buy the land we can apply for the consents. I can't see any reason why the District Council would refuse us if we put up a good case and have plans that comply with all their ordnances. Anyhow, we'll just have to wait and see . . . I enjoyed spending time with your folks today . . . and dinner was fun. George seemed to love the fishing and he was pretty proud to catch the biggest kahawai! Your idea that I should smoke our catch was brilliant. I don't think I've ever seen fish disappear from the plate so quickly! When George was on the old pa site he started quietly chanting something in Maori. I thought he might be calling up the spirits of his ancestors or something!'

'More likely he was saying a karakia for them, Mike.'

'Oh! Yes, you're probably right about that. Anyway we seemed to get along fine. What about you and your mum?'

'She was good too. We talked everything through again, whilst you were off with Dad, and I think she's happy enough now. She knows I am anyway . . . She likes what she has seen of you and our age difference doesn't seem to be bothering either of them. I showed her through the house and she immediately saw why I am looking forward to living there.'

'Well that's all good then isn't it! George was *really* interested in the house. I think he was fascinated by the construction . . . you know, how the logs are all interlocked and so on . . . and he was blown away with the view over the bay. He kept pointing out all the different birds and so on . . .'

'I have a feeling they will want to visit quite often, Mike.'

'Fantastic! There will be heaps of room once we've got the centre started. They'll have their pick of which cabin to stay in.'

* * * * *

Mike woke the next morning to find that Mereana was already up. He got out of bed and turned on the jug to make tea and then looked outside for Mereana. He finally caught sight of her ambling along the beach with her cell phone to her ear.

By the time Mereana came back to the cabin Mike had taken a shower and was just finishing his breakfast.

'Good morning! That was a long phone call,' he commented.

'Two calls actually. I thought I'd better tell Matiu and Huia that we are engaged and that we are going to be seeing them soon!'

'So, a big surprise for them! Were they quite shocked?'

'Surprised at how quickly it has all happened, certainly, but they were both very sweet really. They're delighted they are going to see us soon and they're going to work out some things for us to see and do with them, so I think it's going to be really nice. They said I should say 'Hi' and pass on their congratulations to you, Mike.'

'Are they still enjoying their scholarships?'

'They said they are and I think they are enjoying some independence too, but they were still very happy with the idea of their mum coming to see them!'

'Bound to get a bit homesick from time to time I expect, so seeing you again so soon is going to help . . . What do you think you'll do about Tamati?'

'Hmm. I think I'll just ask Mum to talk about our engagement and the trip at the marae. That way Tamati will get to hear about it. I'll have to talk separately to him at some stage, to sort out what is going to happen to my share of the house, but that can wait I think.'

'Might be a good idea to talk to a lawyer about that and get something drawn up so you can assign your share over to Matiu and Huia. You also need to set something in motion for your divorce I think.'

'I suppose so. How about we arrange to see a lawyer in Motueka when we make our travel bookings?'

'Good thinking! You may as well get things under way . . .'

Chapter 19.

Dear Dad,

Paul and I and everyone here are delighted you are planning to come to London to see us, and of course you must bring Mereana! We can't wait to get to know her and to see you again—this time in much happier circumstances, thank goodness.

Your letter made it clear that the concerns Paul and I had are quite unfounded and that makes us feel so much better. We should never have doubted that you would always act with your usual forethought and wisdom.

We do not have any plans to be out of London in the next two months, except perhaps for a day or two, so you can come whenever it suits you and Mereana. The sooner the better for us, because we are already getting very excited about having you both here.

Don't you dare think about booking separate accommodation! There is plenty of room in my house and you can use the annex bedroom. As you know, it is almost self-contained and will give you whatever privacy you need. It will be no trouble at all to have you stay here, and Jesse and Daniel will be very upset if you go anywhere else! Please stay as long as you wish, because it really won't be any trouble for us to have you—just a real pleasure!

Let us know when you have booked your flights and details of your arrival at Heathrow. Paul and I will be there to meet you!

Jenny and Peter have asked me to pass on their best. We are all talking about organising a special family party to welcome you both!

All our love,
Julia and Paul

Mereana finished reading Mike's letter and gave him a happy grin. 'Looks like we can start planning the trip now, Mike!'

'I'm pleased they are being so positive towards you, Mereana. I didn't really doubt they would be, but I thought they might allow us to stay somewhere else. They aren't going to countenance that, though, are they?'

'Actually, I think it will be lovely to stay with them . . . but it sounds like we can have our privacy too.'

'It's going to be great! We'll make the bookings shall we? There are quite a few options we can consider. The prices vary a lot between airlines and depending on when we decide to fly. There are a couple of travel agents in Motueka where we could find out what the best deals are, so we could do our weekly supermarket shopping over there this week . . . How long do you think we should allow for our time in London, and for Copenhagen and Honolulu?'

'Maybe we should have a couple of weeks in London and, say, two or three days in each of Copenhagen and Honolulu?'

'Sounds good to me . . . We'll probably be away for about a month. I didn't want to be away too long. We have rather a lot on the go here haven't we!'

'There's never a dull moment, that's for sure!'

'I think I might be able to have most of the electrical wiring and plumbing done on the house whilst we are away. I just have to finish framing up all the internal partitions and then they can get started. I should be ready for them in about a fortnight, so we could go then if you like.'

'As soon as that? Wow! I'll have to start thinking about what to pack!'

'Well, don't plan on any more than one suitcase and one carry-on bag. The airlines charge like wounded bulls for excess luggage these days!'

'OK, I'll just have to make sure I have a large suitcase won't I!'

* * * * *

The next day Mereana heard from her friend, Annabelle. She was more than happy to sell her Puponga property to Mereana and Mike, but she wanted to have it valued by a Registered Valuer to see what a fair price would be. She suggested that Mereana and Mike also hire a valuer and proposed that they agree on a price at the mid-point between the two valuations. When Mike heard this he was delighted.

'That's great news, Mereana! I'm more than happy to agree the price on that basis, but we will need to make the purchase conditional on getting District Council consents for what we want to do. Anyway, we can start getting things underway now can't we!'

CHAPTER 20.

6 weeks later

'Good afternoon everyone! This is the Captain speaking. I'd like to welcome you aboard our flight NZ 04, bound for Singapore. All our passengers are now on board and Heathrow Traffic Control has just given us clearance to push back from the gate to commence our journey. We will now secure the aircraft and be on our way. At this stage we anticipate a flight time to Singapore of 12 hours 48 minutes, but I'll be updating you about that and the weather conditions in Singapore later in the flight. In the meantime, I suggest you sit back, relax, and enjoy the in-flight entertainment. Thank you for choosing to fly with Air New Zealand and, once again, welcome aboard!'

'How are you feeling, Mereana?' Mike asked.

'I'm good . . . Getting emotionally prepared for a long flight I suppose. I'm pleased I have a window seat. I enjoy looking out whenever there's something to see.'

'I'm hoping to get a few hours sleep after we have had something to eat.' Mike said. 'Pity the plane is so full. It would have been good to have a spare seat alongside us to provide a bit more room.'

'Never mind. You are probably tired enough to sleep, even if you are a bit cramped for space. With everything we've been doing it will be good to just relax for a while,' Mereana replied.

'Yes, but I find relaxing in an economy class seat is almost impossible . . . for someone my size anyway!'

'You'll be fine, Mike. Put your headphones on and find some soothing music to listen to.'

'That might help . . . It's been a wonderful trip, but I'm pleased to be going home now.'

'It's been a fantastic trip! The places we have been to and the things we have done were just incredible! I know I've seen a lot of it on TV and in movies, but that's nothing like actually being there and experiencing the atmosphere . . . And your family were all so kind and welcoming. I already feel as if they've accepted me. I loved seeing how much they enjoyed having you amongst them, especially the little ones . . . I feel as if I have made a whole group of new friends.'

'They were blown away with you, Mereana . . . No question about that! It *was* lovely to spend time with them and see how they are all getting along. The kids are growing so fast! A highlight for me, too, was seeing Matiu on the way over and then Huia. I hadn't been to Hawaii, or Copenhagen before and I really enjoyed seeing all the sights they showed us. They were pretty rapt to be with their mum again too!'

'They were constantly amazing me by how much confidence and maturity they have gained, Mike. I was really proud of them. They are very happy about us . . . and they can't wait to come to Puponga again when they get home, to see how far we've progressed with everything.'

'Well, let's hope that by then the house will be finished and we are under way with the centre development.'

* * * * *

By the time they had completed the last leg of their long journey and had disembarked from their aircraft at Nelson Airport Mereana and Mike were quite shattered. They had been travelling for thirty hours and the jet lag was starting to take its toll. They couldn't wait to lie down in a regular bed and catch up on some much needed sleep.

Inside the terminal Jenny and George Parata waited to greet them. They had insisted that Mereana and Mike spend the night with them before driving to Puponga.

As they all hugged each other Jenny said, 'You two look as though you could do with some shut-eye! How was the trip?'

'It's been a fantastic trip, Mum!' Mereana replied. 'We've done so much in such a short space of time! It's been like being in a whirlwind! Everyone and everything was fantastic, but it's great to be home. I can't wait to tell you all about it . . . How are you and Dad?'

'We're the same as ever . . . Come on, let's get your bags and we'll go and have something to eat before you collapse. We have some news for you, but I think we should get you back to our place first . . .'

Neither Mereana, nor Mike noticed the look of apprehension on Jenny's face as she made this last comment.

* * * * *

At the house they immediately sat down to eat the smoked chicken salad that Jenny had prepared. Jenny and George had some questions about the time they had spent with Matiu and Huia, but then Mereana remembered that her mother had mentioned some news.

'What was the news you wanted to tell us, Mum?' she asked.

Jenny's expression immediately became grave and she looked at George. He shrugged and spread his hands in a helpless gesture. Mike, noticing the interplay, started to frown and he wondered what was about to be revealed.

'What? What's happened?' Mereana demanded with growing apprehension.

'I'm sorry, Mereana. There's no easy way to say this . . . It's Tamati . . . He had a very bad accident the night before last . . . I'm afraid he was dead when they found him . . .'

'What? Tamati's dead? Oh my Lord! What happened?' Mereana cried out.

As she looked at her parents and saw their deep sadness and concern she realised how upset they were. They had obviously been reluctant to come straight out with such terrible news and its impact was just starting to dawn on her. As Mike moved alongside and took her hand in his she felt a wave of emotion sweep through her and she let out a keening cry as tears began to course down her cheeks.

'Has any one told Matiu, or Huia yet?' she managed to ask in a whisper.

'I think that's something that you must do, Mereana,' George said. 'It wouldn't be right for them to hear about this from anyone else.'

'Oh God . . . They'll be so devastated!'

'Maybe telling them can wait until tomorrow, Mereana,' Mike suggested gently. 'Right now you need to know about the accident and then you need some rest.'

Mereana sat trembling and weeping as George explained what was known about Tamati's accident.

'Tamati has been working so hard to finalise the claim for the Waitangi Tribunal. He has devoted incredibly long hours to it. He was driving home from a meeting at the marae in Motueka when it happened. He was on his own and it seems he must have fallen asleep at the wheel. His car was found smashed into a concrete pillar at the end of the bridge on the Appleby straight. There were no skid marks, so it seems he drove straight into it at quite high speed. The car was badly crunched up . . . kind of folded around the post. Tamati wouldn't have known a thing and his death would have been instantaneous. He certainly didn't suffer . . . Everyone is feeling so bad about it. There was a meeting at the marae yesterday afternoon and a lot of us felt he had been working way too hard to meet the deadline for the claim. We all felt guilty we had let this happen . . . His tangi is going to start the day after tomorrow, Mereana. We are so sorry . . .'

Mereana sat staring fixedly at the table. She felt completely numb. It was so hard to believe this could have happened . . .

'There's something else, Mereana.' Jenny said, rather apologetically. 'I know how hard this must be for you, but you need to know this too . . . Even though everyone at the meeting was so distraught about Tamati we still had to organise his tangi . . . We also had to consider what to do about the claim . . . There's so little time left now . . . Anyway, all the kaumatuas were unanimous, Mereana . . . They want to ask you to finish Tamati's work!'

All Mereana could do was shake her head in disbelief. She couldn't think of any words to say. Mike was feeling incredulous.

'You mean to say that Mereana not only has to deal with Tamati's death and tell her kids they have lost their father, she also has to cope with his tangi and, at the same time, pick up and complete all the work on the claim! Isn't that asking just a bit too much! How can you expect Mereana to cope with all that? I think it's quite unreasonable! Surely there are others who can finish the claim! Mereana will need to arrange for Matiu and Huia to fly home for the tangi and she will need to spend time with them, and then she has things she wants to do in Puponga!'

Neither Jenny, nor George responded to Mike's outburst, but they did look deeply troubled. Finally, the awkward silence was broken by Mereana.

'Mike, I know a lot is being asked of me, but I can see the logic behind it. I know what the key elements of the claim are and I know how Tamati was putting it all together. I am the logical one to pick up what he has done and see it through to a conclusion. It is something I can do for my people . . . I know that there are others who could be asked, but they won't have the inside knowledge that I do, from having been with Tamati when he started this project and, well, for a good deal of the time he worked on it . . . I do feel this is up to me and I'll get it done somehow . . . but right now I need to think about Tamati and Matiu and Huia . . . I'm sorry, Mike, but this is going to mean some changes to our plans . . . I hope you can wait while I see this through?'

'If you really think you need to do this I'll wait for as long as necessary . . . and I'll support you all I can . . . but I'm really concerned how you'll cope . . .'

'If I have your blessing and support, Mike, I'm sure I'll cope . . . I just want to go to bed now and have you hold me until I fall asleep. I'm sorry Mum . . . Dad . . . I have to go now . . .'

* * * * *

The next morning when Mike woke he saw Mereana sitting motionless on a chair by the bedroom window. She was staring out, but Mike could tell she wasn't seeing anything.

'Mereana? Are you OK? How long have you been sitting there?'

'I think I must have woken about an hour ago. I've been trying to think about what I have to prepare for now . . . There's going to be so many things to decide and lots of things to get done . . . I feel as though I'm in of one of those dreams when you can't quite fathom what is happening . . . It's so hard to believe that Tamati is dead. It all seems so unreal. I think I'm in shock . . . I won't be able to go back to Puponga for a while, Mike. I'm sorry, but so much needs to be done here. I'm going to have to move back into our house and get it ready for Matiu and Huia and visitors who will be coming to the tangi. I'll have to stay at the marae during the tangi and then I'll have to start work on finishing the claim. I could be tied up here for quite a few weeks . . . What do you think you'll do, Mike?'

'I'll stay with you of course! I'll try to do as much as I can to take the load off you. Puponga isn't going to go away and the things we were going to do when we got back can wait . . . I will have to go back, just for a day or two, but I want to be here to help whenever I can.'

'You really want to stay on in Nelson, Mike?'

'Definitely! I want to be with you . . . and do whatever you need me to do . . . The things at Puponga aren't really *that* urgent.'

'Well, if you're sure . . . I know I'll manage so much better if you can be my anchor . . . Thank you darling!'

'I'm sure you would do the same for me, Mereana . . . Would you like me to sort out some travel bookings for Matiu and Huia? You'll need to ring them this morning won't you?'

'Yes. I'm dreading that, but I don't have a choice. It would be good if you made the bookings, Mike. Just let me speak to them first. We need to decide how long they should be here.'

'OK. Perhaps we should make a start . . .'

'Give me a cuddle first, Mike . . . It means so much to me, knowing I'll always be able to count on you . . .'

* * * * *

Mereana's telephone calls were heart-wrenching for Mike, even though he could only hear what Mereana was saying. Clearly Matiu and Huia had been deeply shocked and upset by the news. Mereana had been crying quite a lot of the time, but she had still managed to deal with their questions and was able to stress that Tamati had died instantly and had therefore not suffered in any way.

Afterwards she wiped her eyes and looked at Mike sadly.

'They are both very upset, Mike, as you can imagine. They want to come home as soon as you can book a flight for them. Matiu has a lot on, but he thinks he can get away for a week, which will be long enough I think, but Huia wants to come home and stay now. There are only eight more weeks before she was due to come home anyway, so I've told her it will be all right. She can be with us, or with my mum and dad, where-ever she decides, until she goes off to university next year. Anyway, we can sort that out later. So, if you could book a return flight for Matiu and arrange for Huia's December flight to be brought forward that would be good. Flight Centre in Nelson has all their details, but I'd better give them a call to tell them you'll be doing this on my behalf . . . I've told Matiu and Huia we'll email them the flight details as soon as we know. We can do that from Tamati's computer at the house later this morning.'

'OK. I'll ask George if he can take me to pick up my car from the long-term storage yard and then I'll go straight to the travel agent. When I get back we'll go to your place. Is that OK?'

'Sounds good . . . That'll give me time to talk to Mum and ask her what I need to do for the tangi,' Mereana replied.

* * * * *

Mike hadn't seen Mereana's house before and he felt a little odd about the fact that he was going to be living in it for the next few weeks and, probably, sleeping in the bed that Tamati and Mereana had shared. However, he thought he had better get used to the idea and the fact that things were going to be difficult for a while.

The house was in an elevated position on the Tahunanui hills and had an outlook across the airport to Rabbit Island and Tasman Bay. It looked to be about twenty years old and in quite good condition.

'Looks like you have a nice location here, Mereana. What a great outlook! . . . You realise the house will probably be totally yours now?'

'I suppose that's right, assuming Tamati didn't change his Will, but I don't want to think about all that yet. Let's get inside and see what needs to be done.'

'Just tell me where you want me to put our bags and point me in the direction of the computer, so I can email Matiu and Huia and give them details of the flights I've booked for them.'

'I'm so glad you managed to have them meet up and get the same flight from Honolulu, Mike. They'll feel a lot better if they can travel together . . .'

'They'll be here in two days time. Hopefully that will fit in with whatever's going to happen with the tangi?'

'They'll miss the first part, but these things go on for a few days. They'll have plenty of time to be with Tamati and the whanau and their friends.'

'Right . . . How about I go to the supermarket to get some supplies once I've sent the emails? We'll need some food to be going on with and something to offer visitors . . . I'm assuming there will be a few of those over the next day or two . . . .'

'I'm sure there will be, especially my pakeha friends, but most people will go to the marae. They'll know that's where I'll be once the tangi gets under way.'

'Well, I can man the fort here when you need to be away, Mereana.'

'That will be good, but I'll want you with me for the final part.'

'Of course! Just let me know what to do. I want to help as much as possible, but I realise that this is a family thing and there might be a bit of resentment at me showing up, especially from Tamati's family.'

'They will all treat you with respect, Mike. It will be me they may have a problem with, but I'm not going to hide from the fact that we are together now!'

CHAPTER 21.

When word got around the local community that Mereana was at home a constant stream of people called at the Tahunanui house. Friends, teacher colleagues, past students and neighbours all wanted to express their sorrow and best wishes to Mereana. Mike made endless cups of tea and offered a range of cakes, scones and biscuits to the visitors. Mereana greeted everyone with a brave face and took the time to talk briefly with each one before introducing Mike. It was difficult for him recall all the names, or to remember their connection with Mereana, but it was clear that she was held in great regard by them all. He was aware of some curious looks being directed at him, when people thought he wasn't looking, but he kept himself busy and tried to avoid being engaged in any significant conversation. Time enough for that later he thought.

The following day was the start of the tangi, when Tamati would be welcomed on to the marae for the last time. He was to be kept there in an open coffin until the funeral service at the graveside in three days time. Mereana needed to be in attendance throughout the tangi, but she had suggested Mike need only attend the service and burial. Before then, at the marae, family members were expected to stay with Tamati as his mourners were welcomed and gave their tributes to him. They would be speaking directly to Tamati before his spirit departed at the time of his burial. Mike worried about the open coffin, because he thought Mereana would find it a strain to see Tamati lying there as she remained alongside him until the burial. But Maori custom demanded that close family members should stay with Tamati, so he would never be alone before he was buried.

Matiu and Huia missed the first day of the tangi. Mike took Jenny and George to meet them at the airport when they arrived the next morning. He stood back and watched as they greeted their grandparents. It was a very emotional scene, with everyone shedding a lot of tears. He then stepped forward to hug Matiu and Huia and express his condolences.

'We are all going to your house now, so you can have a shower and change your clothes, but then I'll take you and your grandparents to the marae. Your mum is with Tamati and she is waiting for you. She asked that Jenny and George accompany you on to the marae and I guess you will know what happens then. You'll need to take whatever you need for sleeping at the marae, but I want you to know that I am going to be available at any time to pick you up and take you home, or anywhere else, if you have a chance to take a break from the tangi. I'll give you this cell phone, so you can call me whenever you want to. Please let your mum know she can call me too. My cell phone number is programmed into it and of course you know the number at the house.'

Matiu and Huia, looking understandably desolate, just nodded their understanding and they made their way to the baggage claim.

* * * * *

The day Tamati was to be buried turned out fine, but there was a blustery wind from the northwest. Mereana had asked Mike to come to the marae and then drive her, Huia and Matiu to the Marsden Valley Cemetery, where the service and committal was to be held.

Mike arrived just in time to join the last group of mourners to be welcomed onto the marae before Tamati was taken to the hearse and driven to the cemetery. Heni Waaka chanted the karanga, the call of welcome, and the group slowly made their way through the gates and up to the meeting house. A representative of the group Mike had joined went before Tamati's coffin and gave a tribute in Maori. Then it was Mike's turn. He approached the coffin and spoke aloud.

'Tena koe, Tamati. I knew you for just a short time, but that was long enough for me to recognise your intense commitment to the wellbeing and advancement of your people. Your family can be justifiably proud of that and they will always remember how hard you worked for the benefit of others. May you now rest in peace. Haere ra!'

Alongside Tamati, Mereana, Huia and Matiu nodded their thanks to Mike. As he moved away he noticed that Hepera Whatarangi, Maria Kohe and Heni Waaka were among those sitting with the family alongside the coffin. He was glad to see them providing support for Mereana. He then walked back to his car, to wait for Mereana, Huia, and Matiu to join him for the ride to the cemetery.

* * * * *

The funeral service was conducted at the graveside by Hone Ratahi, a Maori Pastor. Matiu, clearly trying hard to put on a brave face, was one of the pall-bearers who set down the coffin, now closed, before the grave. He then stepped back to join Mereana, Huia and Mike at the front of the large assembly of mourners.

Hone opened the service by asking everyone to sing a hymn. This was sung in Maori. Mike knew the tune but not the words, so he just listened as the crowd of about three hundred mourners sang. Their voices were strong and they sang with feeling. Although Mike did not understand the words he was moved by the emotion he felt emanating from the singers. The service was quite short and almost entirely spoken in Maori. There was no need for a eulogy or final tributes. Everything had been said at the marae over the previous days. When Hone said a final karakia and the words of committal Mike had an arm around Mereana's shoulder and he could feel her shuddering with emotion. He glanced at Huia and then Matiu and was pleased to see that Jenny and George were comforting them.

As soon as Mereana had thrown a handful of soil on to the coffin she turned to leave the gravesite and, as Mike led her away, tears ran down her cheeks. Huia, Matiu, Jenny and George followed.

'We're expected to go back to the marae for a while, Mike,' Mereana said. 'There will be some drinks and food there and most people will stay for a short while. I hope it won't go on for too long, because I'm definitely ready to go home!'

'You must be emotionally and physically exhausted, love! You've done so well to keep going . . .'

'I was able to get some sleep, but I feel emotionally drained now.'

* * * * *

In the marae function hall Mike kept himself back from the centre of things. He stood to one side, sipping with a glass of wine, and watched as Mereana, Huia and Matiu spoke to many of the people there. It seemed that most of the people wanted to have a few moments of their time.

'Kia ora, Mike! Good to see you again!'

Mike looked around to see Henare Whataroa smiling at him.

'Tena koe, Henare! It's nice to see you too!'

Henare nodded and then looked serious.

'You said just the right thing when you came on to the marae earlier, Mike. Acknowledging Tamati in that way was appreciated. It must be hard for you to understand how highly regarded Tamati was when you know how he treated Mereana . . .'

'I spoke about the work he did for his people and I do think he deserves recognition for that, Henare. I think it must have been a lot harder for Mereana . . . She had to sit though all those tributes and know that many people probably feel she has been disloyal to Tamati by leaving him . . . But she will never tell them the full story will she!'

'You are right, Mike. Mereana has chosen a heavy load to bear, but she is very strong and she will do it for her children above all else. She doesn't ever want them to find out that Tamati was hitting her.'

'I admire her greatly for that, Henare . . . And now she has to pick up and finish Tamati's work on the claim . . .'

Henare looked at Mike apologetically.

'We *have* asked a great deal of her, Mike . . . I will be the first to acknowledge that, but she is the best person to do it and she knows that herself. She has strength, she has ability, and she already knows a lot about this claim. Now that she has thought about it she knows it is something she wants to do . . . It's very unfortunate we have such a short deadline to meet, but there's nothing we can do about that. The Government has decreed . . . and we have to go along with it . . . Anyhow, I want you to know that your support of Mereana hasn't gone unnoticed, Mike. We all appreciate what you are doing for her. She is much loved in our community you know . . . She obviously thinks the world of you and I think she will gain strength from you, Mike . . . And when the claim has been lodged she will be able to think about Puponga again. I've heard a little about what the two of you are planning and I think it will be fantastic! I look forward to coming over one day to see it all happening!'

'You'll always be welcome, Henare!'

Mike and Henare shook hands warmly as Mereana approached them.

'What are you two up to?' she asked with a smile. 'You look as though you've been plotting something!'

'Not at all! Henare has just been saying nice things about you!' Mike replied.

'That's good to hear! Thank you, Henare!'

Henare grinned.

'It's all true, Mereana! Now I'd better go and see if Hepera is ready to go home. Ka kite . . .'

'Mike, can we go home now? I'll go and ask Huia and Matiu if they are ready to come too, OK?'

'I'm ready when you are . . .'

Chapter 22.

In the three weeks after Tamati's funeral Mereana worked non-stop, finalising the Wakatu-Mohua Claim. She had taken over the living room in the Tahunanui house and piles of papers and files were spread everywhere. Only Mereana knew where everything was. The claim itself was almost ready for printing. It was a casebook that contained hundreds of pages of details about twenty-four separate cases, or events, that had occurred during the colonisation of the Nelson-Golden Bay region after the signing of the Treaty of Waitangi in 1840. These cases recounted breaches of the rights of Maori as set out in the Treaty. Most had occurred before 1860, when the British administration granted The New Zealand Company the right to acquire vast areas of land previously owned by Maori. Much of this land was acquired without first gaining fully informed consent from the Maori owners and without adequate compensation. The result was that, without their land, most of the region's Maori suffered dislocation, loss of their culture and poverty.

Mereana was preparing a combined claim, covering all twenty-four cases, on behalf of and supported by each of the iwis concerned. The facts of each case had to be properly verified, so the claim needed to be accompanied by a 'bank' of separate supporting documents, maps and other evidence, as well as references to all historical publications relied upon as evidence. The claim was to be considered by the Waitangi Tribunal in a formal court-like setting, involving hearings, cross examination of evidence presented and, possibly, visits to locations detailed in the claim. The Tribunal's job was to rule on the veracity of the claim and, if all or part of the claim was accepted, to recommend whether or not the Government should enter into settlement negotiations.

The final section of the claim suggested that the past injustices needed to be publically acknowledged, with a formal Government apology to the claimants and their forebears. It also suggested the types and extent of compensation that would be considered reasonable. This was mostly in the form of land, or other asset, that was held by the State, or could reasonably be expected to be acquired by the State. Mostly, the land was forest, or farmland. The total value of the compensation was inevitably going to be far less than the value of land that had been usurped in the past, because the passage of time and the ongoing settlement and development of the region meant that much of the land in question was no longer under State control. Even if just half of the restitution being proposed was granted by the Government's Office of Treaty Settlements the assets provided would be enough to establish new business enterprises. These would immediately provide additional employment opportunities and eventually provide the income needed to establish new facilities for health and education. The aim was to improve the wellbeing and standard of living of the region's Maori community in the future. For too long members of this community had featured disproportionately in statistics for poor health, low educational achievement, crime and unemployment.

Mereana knew she had just one shot at obtaining the kind of settlement that would allow her people to take a significant step up in relative standard of living and for this to be sustainable for generations to come. She was determined to get it right. Tamati had done all the ground work. He had achieved the backing of each iwi represented in the region. He had set out the nature of each of the twenty-four claims, collated and verified all the historical data and had obtained plans and maps and other reference materials. Now it was up to Mereana to produce the final document, a document of vital importance, because it carried the hopes and aspirations of her people.

Whilst Mereana worked in the living room, Mike took over the dining room. He was using his time in Nelson to prepare a development plan and resource consent applications for the arts and education centre in Puponga, plus a business plan. The business plan needed to set out what the centre was to be used for, how it would be operated and how it would be advertised and promoted. It would also contain financial projections for income and expenditure over a number of years. The development plan would show how the land would be developed, with plans and specifications of buildings, pathways, parking areas, services and landscaping, and set out a construction timetable. Two Resource Consent applications were required. One for the proposed use of the land and the other for the facilities to be established if that use was approved. There was a great deal of work involved and Mike was every bit as busy as Mereana was. He had already arranged for a valuation of Annabelle's property at Puponga and had contacted her to ask which lawyer would be acting for her, and to suggest she initiate her own valuation as soon as possible. He was anxious to proceed with the purchase. He had given Annabelle his lawyer's contact details and advised that the lawyer was fully aware of the likely purchase and would expect to hear from Annabelle's lawyer in due course.

Huia had happily returned to Nayland College to see out the remainder of the academic year and, when she wasn't at college, spent a lot of time studying at home for her end-of-year exams. She wanted to get good passes to enhance her chance of being accepted by Christchurch Teacher Training College. She had decided to follow in her mother's footsteps and become a teacher.

Matiu had stoically returned to Honolulu, just five days after he had arrived back in Nelson for the funeral. He still had another two and a half years of university study ahead of him there and, when he wasn't studying, he had to train for, or compete in middle distance running events. The loss of his father had hit him hard, but he, like Huia, had quickly come to accept Mike as a guide and mentor they could call on; not exactly a father figure, but perhaps the next best thing.

Chapter 23.

The day that Mereana sent the Wakatu-Mohua Claim off to the Waitangi Tribunal was a day of great significance for the tribes involved. It marked the culmination of their efforts to highlight and define past injustices and to seek fair restitution. Now all they could do was to wait for the formal hearing of their claims. They were confident the tribunal would find their claims proven and that it would recommend a settlement process.

Representatives of each iwi had met regularly throughout the period of preparation of the claim and they had 'signed off' on early drafts of each part. The final version of the claim, including Mereana's summation of all of the cases and the proposals for restitution had been circulated to each representative with a request that they immediately propose any last minute changes. When the group met to formally consider the final draft it was unanimously approved and Mereana was roundly congratulated for her work. The enormous contribution Tamati had made was also recognised and acknowledged. Mereana had been quick to point out that she had merely finished off what Tamati had prepared, but she received much praise never-the-less. Everyone knew how much had been asked of her after Tamati's death and she had not failed them.

Pastor Ratahi was called upon to bless the claim documents and he said a karakia on behalf of all the claimants and their forebears. The claim was then boxed up and sent by courier to Wellington.

*****

When Mereana returned home that evening Mike asked her how the final meeting went.

'I'm so relieved, Mike. They approved everything without any problem. I think that was because they had been consulted all the way along the line and they had had plenty of opportunity to make suggestions. I'm so thankful it's over . . . at least for now. We can have our lives back again for a while. It will be weeks and weeks before the hearing gets underway.'

'Did you have a small celebration?'

'Just a short one. Once the claim had been blessed and handed over to the courier we had a drink and some nibbles, but most people were keen to drive home before it got too late . . . and they didn't want to risk being caught for drink-driving.'

'Fair enough, but I hope they gave you some recognition, Mereana. You have worked like a slave to get this all done for them.'

'They were very appreciative, Mike. I'm their golden girl at the moment!'

Mike laughed.

'Quite rightly too! But don't forget that you are my golden girl first and foremost!'

Mereana grinned.

'I can probably just about go along with that . . . But all I feel like doing now is having an early night's sleep and a long lie-in tomorrow.'

'I think you've earned that. How about I give you breakfast in bed before I head over to Tasman District Council to talk to their planning and building engineers?'

'I won't say no to breakfast in bed, Mike, but what do you need to see the engineers for?'

'Oh . . . Well, as you know, whilst you've been slaving away on the claim I have been trying to sort out what we might do over in Puponga. I have some tentative designs for the cabins and the central amenities block. I won't be able to finalise them until we have chosen the sites for each building and checked on what the building codes say we can do, or can't do. I just want to discuss things with them and get their opinion of what I have come up with so far. In the past I have always found that early contact with the people who are going to make the consent decisions is a good practice. When they finally get our applications they'll already know what it's all about and, if they think we have taken notice of their advice, they are more likely to look at our plans positively.'

'That makes a lot of sense, but I want to be in the loop too, Mike.'

'That goes without saying, love. I'm not going to be putting anything forward without you being totally happy with it.'

'How about showing me what you have in mind tomorrow after you get back from the Council. I'll be up and about by then . . .'

'Will do, but you can have a look now if you like.'

'No, I don't think I can concentrate on anything tonight. I feel quite drained and I just want to relax.'

'OK. You should put your feet up and have a nice glass of wine whilst I get the dinner organised,' Mike offered.

'Sounds like a good plan to me . . .'

* * * * *

'How did it go at the Council, Mike?'

'Pretty good! They were very interested in what we are planning. They gave me some useful information and some good ideas, so I think it was well worthwhile going to see them. One of the points they made was to do with the cabins. They thought that what we are proposing might be too much like the motor camp and holiday park just along the road from our place. As you know, that operation is providing caravan and tent sites, plus cheap back-packer accommodation. The planning boys at the Council thought we might need to change our concept a bit to ensure it is substantially different to that existing business. This is because we will need the Council to grant a change of use for our land and people have the right to object to that if they think their interests will be somehow compromised by a change of use. At present our place is zoned for residential purposes only and that doesn't cover the kind of thing we have in mind. If we don't change our concept the Council may go along with any objection they receive from the motor camp, or someone else. So, unless we significantly differentiate our business from the one down the road we probably won't get consent. Our original idea of building cabins without cooking, or bathroom facilities isn't likely to work out, so we should probably look at adding a small en suite and a mini-kitchen to each unit.'

'Won't that cost a whole lot more, Mike?'

'Yes, quite a bit more, but I can see how spending a bit more to add those things would differentiate it from the place down the road *and* make our place appeal to a wider range of visitors as a place to stay. Those who prefer to do their own thing and not use the central facilities can do so, and groups who want to cook and get together communally could still do that. It would mean we wouldn't need to provide shower facilities in the central block and fewer toilets would be needed there, but there's no doubt it will cost more to do it this way. On the positive side, I think we could charge a bit more for the units, so we could compensate for the extra costs that way.'

'Sounds like it will be much more like a motel complex, Mike. I hope it won't become too expensive for the people we want to have at our workshops.'

'I'm thinking we should build accommodation that falls somewhere between a cabin and a motel unit. Perhaps we could call them chalets. I'm pretty sure we could do that and be able to charge less than motel rates. We might be able to offer discounts for group bookings too.'

'I like the idea of calling them chalets, Mike. Perhaps you could design them to have a chalet look about them . . .'

'I can certainly do that. Shall I show you have far I've got with everything now?'

'Yes please. I'm dying to see it all!'

Mike proceeded to show Mereana the work he had done on the business and site plans. The first thing she noticed was the name he had chosen for the arts and education centre.

'I love that name, Mike! Very appropriate! Korimako Lodge has a nice ring to it.'

'I think it's much better to call it Korimako Lodge than say, Korimako Arts and Cultural Centre.'

'Yes! It will be used for a variety of purposes . . . not just arts and culture. So I do think it's better to keep the name a bit more generic, Mike.'

'OK. We'll call it that, for now at least, but let me know if you come up with something better. Now, have a read of my business plan and then we'll take a look at the designs for the chalets and the central facilities.'

Afterwards as they sat down to lunch Mereana said, 'I'm trying hard to be constructively critical of what you have done so far, Mike, but I think you have it all covered superbly well. I'm starting to get excited about this project all over again! I can see I'm going to have to start thinking about my Maori language and culture workshops quite soon.'

'And I'll have to start thinking about my art workshops, but there are a lot of things I have to finalise before we can apply for the consents. Some of those things can only be done in Puponga. We need to work out exactly where everything is going to be sited on the ground for one thing . . . I also think I should go and see the owners of the motor camp down the road and tell them what we are planning. If I do that it might improve the chance that they won't raise an objection when the Council contacts them. They will have the right to object if they feel our proposal will disadvantage them in some way, so I'll try to make it clear that we are not going to be competing against them for their types of customers.'

'OK then . . . Good idea! We don't want to get off-side with anyone do we . . . Letting them know what we want to do before they get the official approach from Council makes a lot of sense to me. Is there anyone else we should talk to as well?'

'No-one I can think of, Mereana. There's no-one else who could possibly be adversely affected as far as I can tell.'

'Fair enough . . . Look, Mike, I can see that you need to go back to Puponga now . . . and I *have* been thinking about when I could go back . . . but it's difficult. I'm not going to be needed for anything more on the claim for the next couple of months, so I don't have to be here for that, but I do have to consider Huia. I know I said she could probably stay with Mum and Dad, but I've been having second thoughts about that. She still has another two months of schooling and needs to do a lot of study for her final year exams. If I'm here with her I think she'll do the work . . . and I can help her. The other thing is I've really enjoyed having her at home again, but I haven't given her much time since she came home from Denmark. I've been way too busy and I feel I've let her down. So I want to make up for that whilst she is still able to be at home.'

'I totally agree, Mereana. I think Huia should be here with you whilst she is still going to Nayland College. After her exams she can come over to Puponga, or stay with your parents, or do a bit of both. But that doesn't need to be decided now . . . The thing is she needs to be here for now . . . and so you need to be here as well! I hope you can make time for some of your writing too! . . . For me, though, I think I need to get back to Puponga to do some more work on the house. The next jobs will be the plastering of the internal walls and tiling the floors. I want to be there to make sure the work is done properly . . . and then I want to get started on the painting. I've kind of given myself an objective to have the house ready to move into by Christmas. I know that isn't really vital, but it would be great to celebrate Christmas and the New Year in our new home . . . And of course I want to finalise our plans for Korimako Lodge, so we can get the consenting process started as soon as possible . . .'

'I understand, Mike. I've been so grateful that you've been able to stay with me here over the past few weeks. It can't have been much fun for you being constantly reminded that this was Tamati's house . . . and me being totally absorbed in the claim. I hate the idea of us not being together all the time, but it won't be for too long and I'm sure I'll be able to come over for most of the weekends. I'll be able to give you a hand with painting then . . . I've been looking forward to doing some of that, because it's something practical I can do to help.'

'That's all decided then! Perhaps I should stay here until the weekend and then go to Puponga. That will give me time to line up a good plasterer and a good tiler. I'm going to have to get professional people to do those jobs . . . and you can help me choose the tiles.'

'How exciting! I've been looking forward to getting involved with the interior decoration. I'll try and see a bit of Mum and Dad whilst you are sorting out the plasterer and so forth. I've been neglecting them for too long. And I need to see my lawyer to find out what is happening about Tamati's estate and what is going to happen to this house.'

'Your parents will be pleased to see you and you can tell George I'm looking forward to taking him back to Fossil Point for a bit of surfcasting when he and your mum come over next time.'

'Boy! You really know how to keep sweet with your in-laws-to-be don't you!'

'Well there's no harm in that! Besides, I enjoy their company . . . What did you have in mind for this place, Mereana?'

'I want to find out about making a Will that provides for the house to pass to Matiu and Huia eventually. In the meantime, though, I think I should arrange for it to be rented out, so we have a regular income from it. What do you think, Mike?'

'Sounds like a good thing to do. You've said there is still a mortgage to be repaid, but you will probably get enough rent to cover that *and* to help with the kid's university fees. I'd suggest you ask your lawyer to recommend a reliable letting agent to take care of everything and regularly check that the tenants are taking good care of the place. You don't want to be worried about all that.'

Chapter 24.

The first thing Mike did when he got back to Puponga was to establish just where each chalet and the central amenities block would be sited. He wanted to identify ten elevated sites for the chalets and have the amenities block in a central position between the chalets and the existing cabin. Mike and Mereana had agreed that the existing cabin could be spruced up and turned into Korimako Lodge's reception and office. The car parking area would be established between the road frontage and the cabin.

Once he had decided on the position of each building Mike took measurements from the fences on the closest boundaries, so that he could pinpoint the exact location on a site plan he was preparing to show the whole development.

When the site plan was finished Mike turned his attention to the plans and specifications for the chalets. They were to be of identical design, providing sleeping for two people, plus a small en suite and basic cooking facilities. He had already worked out the plan and specifications for the amenities block.

At the end of the week Mike was ready to submit his consent applications to the Tasman District Council. He drove back to Nelson to show Mereana what he had done.

'Well, what do you think, Mereana? It's all pretty much as we've already discussed, but it's all down on paper now. If there's anything you think I've missed, or something you would like me to change just say the word.'

Mereana looked at the plans carefully, but decided she should take all of the pages of specifications for granted.

'I think it looks very impressive, Mike. I don't think I can improve on anything really. I like the overall layout and the designs, but I'm a bit lost when it comes to all the specifications and technical stuff . . . I'm pleased you have been able to position everything without having to lose any of the mature trees. So, I think you should go ahead and make the applications.'

'You sure you're happy for me to do that?'

'Yes! As I said it all looks great and I trust you on all the technical stuff. I think you should go and see the Council today.'

'All right! I was hoping you might say that.'

'Oh! Before you go, Mike . . . We have received the two valuations. The one you asked for came this morning and we got Annabelle's one today as well. It came with a letter from Annabelle's lawyer. He says, if we give him the OK, he will draw up an Agreement for Sale and Purchase that is subject to us gaining our consents and with a price mid-way between the two valuations. There was only a $20,000 difference between the two valuations, so I think we can proceed. The price will work out at $320,000.'

'That's great news! The price is about what I was expecting . . . We'll be able to get started on Korimako Lodge as soon as soon as the consents come through in about a month's time! The house should be finished by then . . . Do you think you could ring that lawyer and tell him to go ahead and prepare the documents?'

'OK . . . and I'll ring Annabelle too and tell her it's a done deal provided we get the consents.'

* * * * *

There was a hive of activity at the house over the next six weeks. A joiner came to install the staircase leading from the basement to the living area and, after the plastering of the internal walls of the house was finished, Mike fitted all the skirting boards. The tiler was then able to lay the floor tiles. Painting all the internal walls came next and Mike worked hard on this, using colours that Mereana had selected on one of her weekend visits. Once the internal painting was done the kitchen joinery and bathroom fittings were able to be installed. Mereana had taken the lead in deciding the kitchen layout and bathroom fixtures.

When Mike received word that there had been no objections to his plans for Korimako Lodge and his planning and building consents had been approved and were available for him to uplift he decided to call in to the Council office in Richmond to pick them up. He needed to drive to Nelson anyway to sign the land purchase documents and hand over a cheque for $320,000. Settlement and change of ownership was scheduled for the following week.

After he had finished at the lawyer's office Mike went to his insurance company to arranged replacement cover for the cabin. With all his business then completed he got to the Tahunanui house at 2.00 o'clock and found Mereana busy working on her book.

'I think we have cause to celebrate, Mereana!' Mike said cheerily. 'How about you, Huia and I go out for dinner tonight? I think we should try Boutery's in Richmond. I've read good reports about their menu.'

'What a nice idea! I'm sure Huia will want to come. She loves dining out. It will be nice to come back here afterwards too. You and I haven't been to bed together for two weeks!'

'Hey! Enough of that! You'll have me gobbling my meal down way too fast, just so I can get back here! I'll have indigestion!'

Mereana laughed.

'Well, we could always have an 'appetiser' here and now couldn't we? Huia won't be home from school for another hour . . .'

CHAPTER 25.

Ten days later Mike's electrician returned to put up all the electrical fittings that Mereana had chosen. As this was being done Mike used some time to clear a space at the top of his plot of land where the wind turbine was going to be erected. This was going to supply energy to a bank of batteries being installed in his basement. The batteries, which were also going to be connected to solar panels, were going to provide the power needed for lighting, heating, kitchen appliances and a water pump. The tower for the wind turbine was to be bolted to a heavy concrete pad set into the ground and Mike needed to prepare the site before everything arrived.

Taking a break from his scrub-cutting work Mike looked around. He was surrounded by manuka trees, but right on the highest point of the boundary there was a single lowland beech tree that had somehow missed being felled in the old days when the early settlers had cleared the area for sheep and cattle farming. The tree towered above the manuka that had taken over when the land was allowed to regenerate back to native bush.

On a whim Mike decided to climb the beech tree to see if he could get a 360 degree panoramic view of the area. Once he had managed to clamber up into the lower branches it was relatively easy for him to climb further up to a sturdy looking lateral branch that he could stand on whilst holding onto the trunk. The view from there was stunning! He could see off into the distance in all directions. To the west he could see how the manuka and kanuka cover gave way to grassed farmland stretching all the way to the coast and Tasman Sea. To the north he had a magnificent view of the estuary and local hills, including Old Man Rock, part of a cliff face that looked remarkably like a man's skull. To the south he could see the range of craggy hills that rose up steeply from the shoreline and were covered in thick native forest. And to the east, looking across his own land, he could see the southern side of Farewell Spit and the whole of Golden Bay.

As Mike looked around he realised that he would have to build a lookout up here, alongside the tree he was clinging to. He was sure that visitors to Korimako Lodge would thoroughly enjoy being able to climb up to a viewing platform where they could see for miles and miles in all directions. This was a panorama that deserved to be seen and appreciated. The day was still and clear and, as he continued to gaze about, Mike heard the clear ringing tones of bellbirds off in the distance and the peeping calls of fantails close by. He couldn't discern any man-made noise at all. It was magical! Suddenly, Mike's attention was drawn to a pair of wood pigeons that suddenly appeared from a westerly direction and dropped down into the bush below him. As he tried to see where they had landed he noticed a patch of light green amongst the darker, almost olive green of the kanuka trees.

'Bloody hell! I think that might be another cannabis patch!' he muttered.

As he stared in that direction he picked up the sound of a vehicle approaching. He couldn't see it, because of the thick bush, but it was quite close. He could hear it labouring slowly up the incline and it seemed to be heading towards the patch of lighter green vegetation.

'There must be a track down there,' he thought. 'It probably winds up from the road, somewhere near the estuary.'

Descending from the beech tree, Mike decided to see if he was right about a cannabis patch. He had to make his way through about one hundred metres of dense vegetation. The land dropped away quite steeply, and he had to work hard to avoid slipping and making a noise. There were many tree ferns and a lot of dry brushwood beneath the canopy of kanuka trees. The brushwood could make a loud cracking noise if he stood, or fell on it so he proceeded cautiously, very conscious that he needed to remain unseen.

When Mike saw that he was approaching a cleared area he looked around intently for any sign of stakes or wires that could be part of an alarm system. He was all too aware that Mereana had unwittingly triggered an alarm when she had discovered the cannabis growing up by the old coal mine, but he saw nothing. Then he found himself looking at mature cannabis plants, hundreds of them. As he glanced around he realised that this was quite a large plantation, much bigger than he had been able to see from his vantage point in the beech tree. Just then he heard the murmur of men's voices over to his right and quite nearby. He decided to slip back into the kanuka and circle around in the direction of the voices he had heard. It took him at least ten minutes to move barely fifty metres, but he had to move without a sound and remain under cover.

Again Mike heard voices, very close now. He inched forward to see if he could catch a glimpse of the men. As something moved just ahead of him Mike dropped down behind the trunk of a fallen tree. He could make out what was being said now, something about when the plants should be harvested. As Mike peeked over the tree trunk he saw two men with their backs to him. They were inspecting the plants just ahead of him. There was a tall man wearing jeans and a bush jacket. As he turned to one side Mike saw him in profile. He was probably about thirty-five years of age and was quite tall and lean.

He had sharp features, longish brown hair and a goatee beard. The other man was younger, much shorter and of stocky build. He was rough shaven and was wearing overalls and a beanie. It seemed to Mike that the first man was the boss and the other was probably the one who was looking after the crop.

When the men moved away to inspect more plants off to his left Mike thought he had better make his retreat. He had seen enough.

* * * * *

Back at the caravan Mike grabbed his cell phone and headed across the road to the beach. Fortunately the signal was OK and he was able to make his call.

'Hi Mereana! How are you, love?' . . . Well that's good . . . Look I need to ask you to describe that bloke who was at the Courthouse . . . the one who gave you a bit a fright when we were waiting there. I'm wondering if I might have just seen him over here . . . . Yes that's right. I found another cannabis patch . . . Yeah, I know . . . It's all we need, but we can't ignore it can we!'

As Mike listened to Mereana's description he became convinced that he had just been looking at the same man: tall, lean, narrow face, long hair and a beard.

'He certainly sounds just like one of the men I have just seen inspecting their crop, Mereana. You wouldn't believe how close to our back boundary they are, just a hundred metres down the other side of the hill! I'm going to call Barry Sanders now and tell him he has another job to do out here . . . OK, I'll let you know. Are you still coming over in two days time? . . . Oh good, I'm really missing you . . . It's not the same here when you aren't around . . . I know . . . All right . . . Bye for now, love.'

* * * * *

'Hi, Barry, it's Mike Robinson here. I have another cannabis patch to report. It's just at the back of my place and, twenty minutes ago, there were two men there. They didn't see me, so they may think they are quite safe, but I think one of them may be McCann . . . He fits the description Mereana was given for him anyway . . . Is there any chance you can come out now and take a look? . . . OK . . . How soon can you and your men get here? . . . That would be really good! There's a small chance they might have left before I got back here to ring you, but they seemed to be doing a pretty thorough inspection of the whole crop. I think they will still be there . . . but they might leave within the next hour of course. I can keep a watch on the road if you like. There's only one way out of the area where they are and that's along the road past my place . . . I see . . . Well, if there's only the three of you maybe you could set up a roadblock. I'll be able to tell you if anyone you stop is one of the men who were talking about harvesting the cannabis . . . All right, I'll keep a watch and if I see them drive past I'll ring your office and let them know . . . All right, Barry, I'll see you when you get here.'

Mike was pleased that Barry was prepared to drop everything and head to Puponga immediately. He had been lucky to find him at the station when he had called. Barry had been conducting a weekly briefing session with the three officers who were based with him at Takaka. With any luck three of them would arrive in under an hour. Mike decided to go to the cabin to get his camera, so he could photograph any vehicles that drove south past his gate before the Policemen arrived. Hopefully he could get the licence plates in his shots.

* * * * *

Only four cars had passed by before Sergeant Barry Sanders arrived with two of his officers. They were in two vehicles, one of which was a van that could transport prisoners.

'Hi there, Barry! I think they might still be up there . . . There have been four cars drive by, but I didn't recognise anyone in them. You'll have a chance to apprehend them I think.'

'As I told you, Mike, we haven't got the manpower to try to contain them up where they are growing the stuff at this short notice, so we'll try your idea of a road block. I noticed a spot about eighty metres south of here where we can conceal the van, and we'll have my car just inside your driveway if that's OK. Both locations are bush-lined, so anyone driving by won't be able to see us before they reach our position. Once they get to the driveway here I'll alert Jeff and he'll immediately drive out from his position to block off the road. I'll do the same, to deter them from thinking of turning back. It's the best we can do at short notice and without a full team of us, but maybe we'll get lucky . . . They could attempt to drive round the van, but we'll have road spikes set up to stop them if they try that. They won't get away by vehicle, but if they make a run for it on foot and head into the undergrowth we might have a job catching them . . . We'll have to take our chances on that . . . Now, we need to get set up right away!'

The two Constables who were waiting in the van headed back down the road to set out the road spikes and then take up their position at the spot Barry had mentioned. Barry positioned his car in Mike's driveway and sat there with his engine idling whilst Mike stood just inside his gate, where he could spot anyone approaching from the north. He still had his camera and was determined to photograph whoever came by. There was no activity for a while and Mike glanced back down the road to see if he could see any sign of the Police van. He couldn't, but he noticed the Constables had set up a barricade across one half of the road.

'I see your boys have set up a partial road block down there, Barry,' Mike said.

'That's right. Anyone coming from the south will still be able to drive through, but if someone comes from the north we'll block the gap. If they try to go through the barricade they'll end up on our spikes,' Barry replied.

Just then Mike heard the sound of a vehicle driving south towards them.

'Someone's coming, Barry!'

Barry immediately used his mobile radio to contact his men.

'TCR 2, stand by!' Barry warned them.

A silver-grey Ute came into sight and Mike took a snapshot of it with his camera. As it came alongside the drive Barry radio'd instructions.

'TCR 2, go! Get out there now!'

Mike was able to see the driver reasonably well and as Barry drove out to block the road with his car he called out.

'I think it's them, Barry!'

Down the road the Police van had appeared and one of the Constables was standing on the centre-line and holding up his hand to signal the Ute to stop. It did, but it was well back from the barricade. For a moment or two nothing happened. Then the Ute suddenly accelerated forwards. The Constable had to throw himself sideways to avoid being hit as the Ute swerved around the van and crashed through the barricade. Two seconds later, as it passed over the spikes, its tires instantaneously deflated. It skidded left and ploughed into a low bank at the side of the road. A moment later the driver's door of the Ute swung open. A man jumped out and raced across the road. He vanished into the dense undergrowth that ran alongside the road and up the hill. The Constable picked himself up from the road and set off in pursuit, but his quarry already had a forty metre start on him.

At the same time the second Constable left the van and ran towards the Ute. The passenger door opened . . . The second man emerged slowly. He was short and stocky and had his hands help up in submission. He was quickly cuffed and led to the Police van where he was formally arrested and had his rights explained before he was locked inside. Barry Sanders arrived at the van at that point and, seeing that his help wasn't needed there, he reached for his radio.

'TCR 3, receiving?'

'Three receiving . . . I've lost him for the minute. I think he's lying low somewhere, because I can't hear him moving.'

'What's it like in there?'

'Pretty difficult, boss. It's very dense scrub, lots of ferns and vines under the trees . . . Really difficult to see clearly for more than a few metres and I can't see any sign of which way he headed . . . Very easy for someone to hide in here I'm afraid.'

'All right, if you can't see where he is or which way he went, come on out. We don't know if he's got any sort of weapon and there's no point in putting you in any danger.'

The Constable arrived back at the roadblock at the same time as Mike.

'Sorry, Boss. He was pretty quick and I lost him within about fifty metres. It's very overgrown in there and he could be anywhere.'

'Not to worry. At least we collared one of them . . . and we've got the vehicle,' Barry replied.

'And you have some photos,' Mike said as he waved his camera. 'I managed to get a shot of him as he ran from the Ute. I also got a shot of the other chap with his hands up.'

'Let's have a look at the one who scarpered, Mike,' Barry suggested.

The image of the man on the small screen on Mike's digital camera was slightly blurred, but it seemed that it would be sufficient for identification purposes.

'Does that look like the man you saw at the cannabis patch, Mike?' Barry asked.

'I'd say so, but I can probably be more definite if I download the picture to my laptop and have a look at it on that. The fellow in the van is definitely one of the two I saw earlier.'

'OK. Do you have your laptop here, Mike?'

'It's in the cabin. Shall I go and do the download?'

'Yes please. I'll come along shortly . . . Now, Jeff, I'll get you and Dave to clean up here. The Ute can stay where it is. It's not driveable, but we need to lock it up and take the number plates and keys, in case our man comes back to it later. Be careful what you touch. We'll need to come back tomorrow to recover it and take it in for fingerprints and so forth. Once you've done that I'll get you to drive south for a bit and then lay up somewhere where you can't be seen, in case our second man decides to take a walk home. While you are waiting you can call in for a vehicle check. I want to know who this Ute is registered to. I'll go and see what photos Mike has been able to take now and then get him to show me the cannabis patch. It's unlikely, but I want to see if they have left someone there. If you haven't seen the guy who took a runner by the time I reach your position down the road we'll call it a day out here. We'll process the man we have and do all the usual follow-up work back at the station.'

* * * * *

At the cabin Mike and Barry were peering at the laptop computer screen.

'That's definitely the man I saw at the cannabis patch, Barry. I reckon he might be this McCann chap.'

'It's him all right, Mike. He's the one the CIB boys have had in their sights for years. He matches the description perfectly I'd say. Well done, Mike! You and your camera could be just what we need to wrap this up and put these guys away!'

'You'll have to catch McCann first, Barry.'

'We'll get him. It's only a question of when, not if. And when we do, with your evidence, there's no doubt he'll be going to jail . . . Now, you better show me where the cannabis is, Mike. I'll take a quiet look around and make sure there's no-one else out here we need to know about.'

Mike led Barry up to the back of his land and then down through the kanuka trees and ferns to the edge of the cannabis patch where he had seen McCann and his accomplice.

'Best wait here, Mike, whilst I quietly circle around and see if anyone's here. I'll give a whistle if the coast is clear and you can come and join me.'

'I'm a bit worried that McCann might have made his way back here, Barry. Don't you think it would be better if we stayed together?'

'It's possible he might have come here, but I doubt it. He'll know we are on to this operation now and he will keep well away I should think. But maybe you're right; if you are prepared to tag along I'd appreciate your support. Just move as quietly as you can and keep your eyes skinned for booby traps!'

The cannabis patch was deserted and they saw no sign of any alarm system, or booby traps. They found a very overgrown track leading down the hill in a northerly direction and there were clear signs it had been used recently.

'This is going to be quite a haul, Mike. There's a helluva lot of cannabis here! It's well hidden away though. There's no way anyone would ever see it, except from a low flying helicopter.'

'Or from up a tall tree, Barry!'

'Oh yes, I'd forgotten that was how you spotted it! Look, I think we should follow this track down to the road. I want to know just where the turn-off is, so I can show the team when we come back tomorrow. Well be taking photos and measuring up and so on, and then we'll pull all this stuff out of the ground and take it away.'

When they got back to the cabin Mike said, 'I'm quite worried about McCann, Barry. He doesn't seem the type to ignore anyone who has put his business in jeopardy. It was almost certainly him who arranged for that dead sheep to be planted in our cabin and for Mereana's car to be wrecked.'

'It's a pity he was able to elude us this time, Mike, but there was always a chance he would. We didn't have the men we needed to cover all eventualities. I think it was important to move quickly, so it was a matter of doing the best we could with only the three of us. We did get the other chap and the vehicle and we have your evidence and photos. That's a whole lot that we didn't have before! Plus we will be destroying the crop. It's worked out pretty well all things considered.'

'I understand that, Barry, and I am not questioning your decisions or anything. It's just that this McCann is obviously a nasty piece of work and he has already shown how vindictive he can be. He could have been quietly watching us whilst we were checking out his cannabis patch. If he was there somewhere he'll know I am the one who has stuffed things up for him . . . and that cannabis must be worth many thousands of dollars. He'll be as mad as hell!'

'I take your point, Mike. The guy could have seen us, or he may be well away from this area now. He could decide to get back at you and if he does try to do that I'm not sure there's a lot we could do . . . I don't have the resources to station a man here for your protection. Perhaps you should consider leaving the area for a while, Mike, just in case . . .'

'I don't think that's much of an option . . . It could be months before you find him. I couldn't stay somewhere else indefinitely, or until you catch him. I've got things to do here!'

'Well, maybe we can set up a daily check when you phone in to the station to let us know you are OK. If you miss a scheduled call we'll hot-foot it out here to see what's happened.'

'I suppose that's better than nothing, but I really hope you can nab this guy quickly!'

'We'll be doing our best Mike and the CIB and Motueka Police will be looking for him too.'

'Fair enough . . . What time should I phone in each day?'

'Let's make it at midday. I'll tell our receptionist to be waiting for your call and to let me know immediately if she doesn't hear from you.'

Barry got into his car, but he signalled Mike to wait for a moment whilst he used the car's radio.

'TCR 1 to TCR 2 over.'

'Two receiving, boss. No sign of our man. It looks like it *is* McCann. The Ute is registered to him. Are you on your way now?'

'I'm just leaving. Pull in behind me when you see me pass your position and we'll get our prisoner back to the station . . . Out.'

'No joy then, Barry?' Mike asked.

'They haven't seen him, not that I really expected them to. You got it right, Mike. It *is* McCann. The boys ran a check and found out the Ute belongs to him. He'll be laying very low somewhere and it's not worth trying to wait him out. Chances are he will be avoiding the road anyhow. I think he's bound to have a cell phone, so he has probably called for someone to come and pick him up at some remote spot. I could suggest that the Motueka boys put up a roadblock on the Takaka hill, and stop and search all vehicles, but I'm sure they wouldn't be able to spare the manpower for that, especially when we have no idea when McCann might try to return to Motueka. It would be better for them to check out all his haunts and known associates in the next day or two, and see if they can find him that way. Anyway, I'll see you tomorrow, Mike.'

'OK. Cheers, Barry.'

Mike frowned in frustration as he walked up to the cabin. He felt strangely vulnerable, knowing that McCann was out there somewhere and that he might now be fully aware of who had called in the Police. But then he had an idea and smiled. Cannabis growers weren't the only ones who could set up alarm systems!

The alarm system that Mike devised that evening was crude, but it worked. He used nylon fishing line, wooden pegs, a pulley, six large steel bolts and some old tubular-steel wind chimes. He suspended the pulley and wind chimes from the eave just outside the cabin door and, using the fishing line and the wooden pegs, he fashioned a trip wire to run all around and out from the cabin at ankle height. He then took one end of the line up to and through the pulley and then tied it to the steel bolts, so that they hung just below the chimes. Mike's idea was that, if someone walked into the trip wire it would cause the bolts, which were wired together in a cluster, to be pulled up into the group of suspended wind chimes. The jangle of sound created would signal the presence of an intruder. He tried it out a couple of times and it worked well. The nylon line was hard to see even in daylight and, by a process of trial and error, Mike had worked out that six bolts suspended from the pulley provided just enough tension on the line. Feeling much happier, now that he had an early warning system, Mike took his cell phone across to the beach to call Mereana and tell her all about the day's events.

Back up the hill, hidden amongst the kanuka and tree ferns, Kenny McCann looked on and chuckled as Mike crossed the road.

'Think you're safe now do you?' he muttered. 'No-one causes me all this shit without pay-back . . . You are about to find out that being such a do-gooder, interfering bastard is going to cost you big time!'

Chapter 26.

Mike woke with a start. He wondered what had caused him to suddenly jerk into wakefulness. He didn't think he'd been dreaming, so he sat up and listened. Hearing nothing, he shrugged and settled down to sleep again. No doubt his alarm would have sounded if anyone had come up to the cabin.

The next time Mike woke he was startled to see a red glow at the bedroom window. He jumped out of bed to investigate. He ran from the bedroom and immediately saw the red glow at all the other windows too! When he looked out from the kitchen window he saw a wall of flames! He ran to another window and then another. There were flames all around the cabin and they were as high as the eaves! Suddenly there was a loud crash as a large rock smashed through the kitchen window and landed on the floor in front of him.

'Bloody McCann!' he thought . . . and then, 'Have to get out!'

Mike raced back into the bedroom and took a few seconds to pull on some shoes and his jeans. He then grabbed a blanket off the bed and took it to the shower. He quickly doused the blanket in cold water and was about to wrap it around his body when he had a sudden thought. He needed to take his camera! It contained evidence to convict McCann. He ran to the dining room and grabbed the camera and also his laptop. The laptop contained all his plans for Korimako Lodge. Then, feeling he couldn't wait another moment, he covered himself in the wet blanket, opened the front door and ran out through the flames to the darkness beyond.

Once he realised he was clear of immediate danger Mike unwrapped himself from the blanket and looked back at the cabin. It was well alight. Flames encircled the whole cabin and were now reaching above the level of the eaves. Mike quickly realised that the walls of the cabin must have been doused with petrol, or kerosene. The spread of the fire was too uniform, and the blaze too fierce, for any kind of accidental cause. Then he heard the sound of breaking glass as tremendous heat took its toll on one of the bedroom windows.

Standing behind some bushes at the roadside McCann smiled in satisfaction. He had taken the risk of cutting the trip wire and had been pleased that the only sound was a thump as something fell onto the deck. He had held his breath, waiting to see if the noise had disturbed anyone, but everything had remained quiet. After a few minutes he proceeded with his plan. He had retrieved a 20 litre can of petrol from the tray of his Ute and had quietly poured the fuel along the base of all four walls of the cabin. Once he had thrown a lighted match to ignite it he stood back and watched as the fire took hold. When he was satisfied that the cabin was well ablaze he had thrown a hefty rock through a window, hoping this would create enough noise to warn those inside and allow them enough time to make their escape. As he'd continued to watch he had been surprised at how quickly the fire had escalated and had begun to worry that his warning might have come too late. He didn't have murder in mind, but he did want to destroy his tormentor's cabin and give him a major fright! Now, seeing that his plan had worked perfectly, he turned and walked away. It was time to make his way to Pakawau where he had arranged to meet up with a dealer he had called on to give him a ride back to Motueka.

Mike instinctively knew that the cabin could not be saved. It would take a fire engine at least half an hour to get from Collingwood to Puponga and, at that time of night, probably longer. By that time there would be little left. He ran around to the back of the cabin where there was a garden hose. He thought he might be able to douse some of the flames with that, but found he couldn't get close enough to the cabin to operate the tap mounted on the back wall. All he could do was watch helplessly as the cabin burned unabated, and think how fortunate he had been to get out unharmed. If he hadn't woken and jumped out of bed when he had, before the brick had smashed through the kitchen window, he could easily have been overcome by smoke, or badly burned. The fire had swept into the cabin almost immediately after he had made his escape . . .

Mike realised he should make a 111 call. He wanted the emergency operator to alert the Collingwood Volunteer Fire Brigade and inform the Takaka Police, so he decided to run to the nearest occupied house to wake someone.

It seemed to take ages to rouse the old fellow who lived in the nearest house. When he finally came to the door Mike explained his situation and he was quickly allowed to make the call.

* * * * *

The next morning Mike emerged from his caravan early and went to survey the remains of the fire. The cabin and all its contents had been reduced to a stinking mound of soggy ash. Nothing had survived. Mike sighed deeply and headed along the road to ask if he use the old fellow's phone again.

'Good morning, Ted. I was wondering if I could make one more phone call?'

'Sure. Come on in. You want a cuppa whilst you're here? You probably need something . . . Not much left of your place is there!'

'I've just had a coffee thanks. I was lucky to still have some supplies in my caravan. I'll just make the call and then get out of your hair if that's all right. I've got quite a lot to do today.'

'I can imagine! Well you go ahead. You know where the phone is . . .'

'Thanks Ted, I appreciate it!'

* * * * *

'Hi, Huia! It's Mike here. Can I talk to your mum please? . . . Hi, Mereana! I'm afraid I've got some bad news. The cabin was set alight last night. I'm afraid it's a total write-off . . . and we've only owned it for two days! . . . Yes, I'm OK . . . a bit lucky to get out before it was too late . . . . Yes, I'm fine really . . . I covered myself with a wet blanket to make sure I didn't get burnt . . . . No, I wasn't even singed! . . . No, there's absolutely nothing of the cabin left standing . . . Just as well I took out the insurance cover last week, but our possessions inside were lost too and I'm afraid they weren't covered. I didn't think we'd need contents insurance as well, seeing as we aren't going to be living in it after another week or so. I still had some clothes over in the caravan, so I'm OK for now. I did manage to save my camera and laptop, but I don't have a cell phone anymore and there's no food . . . I'm ringing from Ted's house along the road . . . . Well it was definitely arson. No question about that! I'm sure it was that McCann bastard . . . The Collingwood Fire Brigade arrived as soon as they could, but all they could do was damp down the embers really. I'm expecting the Police will show up shortly . . . I told you they were coming to sort out the cannabis over the hill . . . Well, when they see what's happened here, they'll have some more motivation to catch McCann . . . . Yes, that's right . . . Look, I was wondering if you could come over today, instead of tomorrow as planned. I assume Huia has netball on Saturday and wasn't going to be coming with you? . . . Maybe she could go to your parents for an extra night this time. Would that be possible? . . . OK, great. Would you mind picking up a new cell phone for me? I'm with Vodafone, so if you go into their shop in Richmond they should be able to put a replacement Sim card into a new phone for me and maintain my present number and call plan . . . . I'll leave it to you to pick something, love . . . I don't need all the bells and whistles though . . . A basic phone will do just fine . . . . OK, and can you get some food supplies from the supermarket? I've only got tea and coffee in the caravan now . . . I'm going to have to go to Collingwood to get something for brunch later, after I have seen Barry Sanders . . . . OK, love, I'll see you around five o'clock and I'll tell you more about what's happened then. Love you . . . Bye for now . . .'

* * * * *

A short while later Sergeant Barry Sanders called in on his way to the cannabis plantation.

'I heard you had a spot of trouble, Mike.'

'Yeah. McCann trouble!'

'You reckon?'

'I'm pretty damn certain, Barry. I was lucky to wake up just after midnight and notice an orange glow coming through the window. The whole of the outside was alight and I had to cover myself in a wet blanket to get through the flames. I was very lucky to get out when I did, because it was amazing how quickly it took hold. It was obvious that petrol was poured along all the walls, because every part of the cabin was on fire and all the flames were equally intense. There's no way it would be like that if the fire started in one localised part of the building. I discussed it with the firemen when they were here and I'm sure they all thought it was arson. There's an investigator coming out later to officially determine the cause of the blaze, but there really isn't any doubt . . . and I found a petrol can that's definitely not ours!

'There's something else you should know . . . After you left yesterday I was worried that McCann might still be about, so I rigged up an alarm system, with a tripwire right around the cabin. You can still see the remains of it there. I've had a look at it and I can see that it was cut. I reckon McCann must have seen me rigging it up. He would have cut the line so he could walk around with his petrol can without setting the alarm off. It wouldn't have worked once the fire melted the nylon cord I used for the tripwire, but McCann had obviously decided to warn me. He threw a large rock through the kitchen window . . . He left it pretty late, though, because the cabin was completely enveloped in fire by that stage. Fortunately for me, I was already up by then and about to make my escape . . . I don't want to think about what might have happened if I hadn't got out then. I probably surprised McCann, because it was only a few seconds after the rock came in through the window that I escaped. He must have been pretty close by at that point. I think he would have waited to see if I made it out OK.'

'Hmm. Maybe he didn't want a death on his conscience, but he was obviously determined to get back at you, Mike, like you thought he might. I'm sorry he succeeded the way he has. It must have been a shock for you to find the whole place alight, and it sounds as if you could have been in big trouble if you hadn't got out when you did. You're lucky you weren't badly hurt!'

'You can say that again! I did manage to save two items though, Barry, so maybe I'll have the last laugh yet . . .'

'Oh yes? What did you save?'

'My camera and my laptop.'

'Oh, I see! Good for you, Mike . . . We still have your photos!'

'Yes . . . and I'll be emailing them to you as soon as I have your email address, Barry.'

'Good thinking! Now, you'd better show me the petrol can you found. We'll need to have it checked for fingerprints . . .'

'I left it where I found it, Barry, and I didn't touch it. It's over there at the edge of the manuka . . . but I couldn't see the cap anywhere.

* * * * *

Mereana arrived at the caravan just after five o'clock and immediately made a big fuss of Mike.

'My God, Mike! It must have been such a shock to wake up and find the whole cabin was on fire! I'm hugely relieved that nothing happened to you! You were so lucky to get out unscathed! How are you feeling now?'

'Just angry . . . and frustrated that McCann is still on the loose. Come and see what's left of the cabin, Mereana. We can unload the groceries shortly.'

* * * * *

'My goodness! There's not much more than a pile of ash left! I don't know quite what I expected to see, a fire damaged building I guess . . . but this is just . . . total annihilation!'

'I'm sorry about all the stuff you've lost, Mereana.'

'Oh, I can do without a few clothes and some bedding . . . and most of the rest was Annebelle's . . . but of course we bought all that didn't we?'

'Yes. We purchased the land, building *and* contents . . . just three days ago! . . . At least we'll get an insurance payout for the cabin. In some ways it might end up *not* being too big a deal that we've lost the cabin, because I think we can use the insurance money to build an additional chalet. We could build it where the cabin was and use it for the reception and office . . . It could end up being a better option than the cabin.'

'That would be a good idea and I think a new chalet would look a whole lot better than the old cabin . . . I know this is all something we could have done without, Mike, but I am pleased it didn't happen whilst Annabelle still owned the place. I would have felt absolutely awful if I'd had to tell her it had burnt to the ground whilst she was letting us use it.'

'Well that's something I suppose. Come on, we'll go and unload the groceries. I'm starving!'

CHAPTER 27.

Kenny McCann knew he was in serious trouble and that the Police were making a big effort to try to find him. He kept getting reports of this from the men who worked for him. They were feeling seriously hassled when Police turned up to question them and search their premises. He understood he was finished in Motueka and was trying to find a way to get to Australia without alerting the authorities. He had plenty of money and thought he might be able to bribe some ship's crew to hide him on board during a passage across the Tasman Sea. In the meantime he was hiding out in a sleep-out at the back of an old friend's property in Motueka. He had taken the chance that the cops would not think to look for him at Bevan Miller's house, because Bevan was not one of his known associates in the drug trade. They had been schoolmates, and had kept in touch occasionally, but Bevan was not part of the group that Kenny usually socialised with and he had never been involved in his criminal activities. He had a clean record and legitimate work at one of the local orchards. Bevan was well aware that Kenny was behind most of the drug trade in the region, so he hadn't been happy to have Kenny stay in the sleep-out. He didn't want to be caught up in anything Kenny had going on, but Kenny had befriended him and protected him when he had been bullied at school. He thought he owed Kenny a favour for this. Anyway, Kenny had assured him he only wanted to stay in the sleep-out for a few days, until he moved permanently to Australia. And Kenny convinced him that, because he would not use the sleep-out for any 'business', there was no risk in letting him stay there.

McCann was sitting by a window in the sleep-out, checking the shipping column in a three-day-old newspaper, when he noticed a policeman come round the side of Bevan's house and go to knock on the back door. He cursed to himself, quickly stood up, backed away from the window, and grabbed a jacket, his wallet and his cell phone. He was sure that another policeman would be simultaneously trying the front door. As Bevan was at work McCann knew the Police would have no response to their knocking, but he expected they would start looking around the property and would be coming to check the sleep-out within the next couple of minutes. He needed to make his escape quickly!

Having no response to his knocking on the back door the policeman returned to the corner of the house and waited there. He was obviously making sure that no-one could slip away from the rear of the house without being seen. McCann saw him look towards the sleep-out, but then he turned towards the road, presumably waiting for his colleague to put in an appearance. As soon as McCann saw that the policeman had his back to him he quietly opened the door and made a run for the back fence. He leapt up to grab the top of the fence and heave himself up, but he must have made some noise because he was spotted just as he was about to drop into the neighbouring park.

'Hey, you! Stay right where you are!' the policeman called out.

McCann didn't hesitate. He dropped and ran. He sprinted across the park to the next street, crossed over and headed towards a side street. Looking back he saw no sign of pursuit so, to avoid drawing attention, he slowed to a fast walk. He began to think of where he could hide whilst he used his cell phone to call an associate to pick him up. He decided to make for the rugby ground two blocks away and take shelter in the toilets there. He was relieved that no-one else was walking the streets and he took cover whenever he saw a vehicle approaching. He was lucky not to be spotted when a police patrol car suddenly surged around a corner. He quickly stepped into a sheltered driveway until the car raced by. It seemed to be headed towards Bevan's house. Then, walking quickly, he turned into the street that led to the rear of Rugby Park.

The rugby ground was deserted when he arrived and as he entered the men's toilet block he breathed a sigh of relief.

'Doug? Kenny here . . . I need you to come and pick me up pronto! The cops are on to me! They turned up at my mate's place and I barely got away. They'll be organising an all-out search right now and they know roughly where I am. I have to get away from Motueka and it has to be right this minute! Drop everything and come now! I'm in the men's toilets at Rugby Park. Be quick! . . . OK . . . Hurry!'

Three hundred metres away Police Dog Jess was closing in. The Alsatian's handler had been one of the policemen sent to check the Miller house. Seeing McCann disappear over the back fence he had raced to get Jess from his van and set her on McCann's trail. He hoisted her over the back fence and she quickly started tracking.

McCann was still waiting for Doug to pick him up when he saw two patrol cars stop just outside the main entrance to Rugby Park. He realised there was no way Doug could get to him now. He had to start running again. He burst out of the toilets and dashed along the side of the grandstand, hoping he could duck around the side of it and into the back yard of a neighbouring house. As he ran he glanced over his shoulder and saw a policeman signalling to his colleagues and pointing in his direction.

'Stop where you are!' the policeman shouted.

McCann took no notice and tried to run even faster. As he reached the end of the grandstand he glanced back again. To his horror a large Alsatian was racing after him! Five seconds later the dog had seized McCann's arm and was growling ferociously. It felt as though his arm was being pulled out of its socket and that the animal's teeth were imbedded deep into his flesh. There was nothing McCann could do except cry out.

'Call the bloody dog off, for Christ's sake! Aargh! Shit! . . . Make it let go!'

To McCann it seemed ages before the policemen arrived. He couldn't believe the strength of the dog as it tugged and shook his arm fiercely.

'Get down on the ground you! Face down!' a policeman instructed.

As McCann dropped down to comply another command was given.

'Good girl, Jess! Heel!'

Immediately the dog released McCann's arm and started to bark triumphantly as she returned to her handler's side.

'Good girl, Jess! Quiet now.'

As McCann lay there gasping in pain first one arm and then the other was pulled up behind his back and he was hand-cuffed and checked for any weapon he might be carrying.

'Aargh, Christ! My arm! My shoulder!'

'Serves you right, McCann! You were told to stop running. Let's get you into the wagon and off to the Station. We'll get you patched up there and, before you're locked away in one of our lovely cells, we'll have a little chat about what you've been up to. You'll find our cells are a very basic form of accommodation, but you'll need to get used to that. I'm sure you won't be going home anytime soon my son!'

CHAPTER 28.

Mike took his cell phone to the beach to make two calls. He checked to see if he had a signal and then dialled the number he had written down for the Takaka Police Station.

'Can I speak to Sergeant Sanders please? . . . Thank you . . . . It's Mike Robinson here, Barry. I was wondering how things were progressing with this McCann business. Anyway, how are things with you?'

'I'm fine, Mike. Actually Jeff and I were just about to come and see you. I was going to give you some news when we got there, but I can tell you now. The CIB and the Motueka boys caught Kenny McCann yesterday. He's appearing in Court today to be formally charged with cannabis offences. Bail will be opposed, because we think he's a flight risk and because he is suspected of the arson at your cabin.'

'Hey! That's great news, Barry. Mereana and I will be greatly relieved that he is finally out of circulation!'

'Yes, well how long he's out of circulation will depend on what we can prove he's been doing. We can definitely prove he was involved with the cannabis behind your place, but we'd really like to get him for the arson too. Unfortunately there were no prints on that petrol can. He must have wiped it clean. So Jeff and I are going to come out there to see if we can find the cap that was missing when you found the can. I'm hoping McCann tossed it away somewhere nearby and that he might not have thought to wipe it clean first. Unless we can find it, with his prints on it, I don't think we'll be able to prove he set the cabin alight.'

'I see . . . OK, I'll give you a hand with the search, Barry.'

'Thanks, Mike. We should be there in about forty minutes. Bye!'

* * * * *

'Hi darling! How are you? . . . I'm good and I'm missing you too! I've got some good news, love. Kenny McCann's been arrested! . . . Yeah, it's a big load off my mind too! . . . Barry Sanders is on his way here now, to see if he can find the cap to that petrol can. Without that and without finding McCann's fingerprints on it, he says they won't be able to charge him with arson . . . . Yes, I hope so too. The longer he can be put away the better. Have you heard from Matiu? . . . Oh, I'm really pleased! I know he was building up for that race. It's great to hear he had the win. What about Huia? . . . Hey! Being selected for the rep. team is a pretty big deal! She must be pretty good! I'll text them both and give them my congratulations. And what about you love? Have you been able to do much writing this week? . . . Hmm, sounds like you need to come over here for a bit . . . You know . . . soak up the atmosphere and get some inspiration . . . . Yeah, you know I'll try anything don't you, but OK, I'll try to be patient and wait until next week! Love you . . .'

* * * * *

Sergeant Barry Sanders, Constable Jeff Roberts and Mike were standing at the roadside by the driveway that used to lead to the cabin.

'How do we go about this search, Barry?' Mike asked.

'To start with I think we should try to work out where McCann might have been and what he might have done when he was setting your cabin alight. From what we know it happened after midnight. It would have been completely dark. There's no street lighting and you didn't have any house lights on at that time. So, if I was McCann, I'd feel pretty safe going onto the road and getting the can of petrol from the Ute. Then he probably just walked in here through the front gate. If you are right about him cutting your alarm system I think he would have put the can down somewhere close to where he made the cut. Where was that exactly, Mike?'

'Just off to the left there. It was about two metres yards from the side wall of the cabin.'

'OK, let's go to that point . . .'

The three men moved to the spot.

'OK,' Barry said. 'So, if he put the can down whilst he cut the trip wire, what would he have done next? . . . I think he would be concerned to do what he planned and then get away as quickly as he could, don't you?'

'That makes sense, boss,' Jeff said. 'No point in him waiting around at that stage . . .'

'Well let's assume that he got straight on with it. I think he would have taken the cap off the can right here. That type of petrol can has one of those safety caps you need press down to release, before you can unscrew it. It would have been easier to do that if the can was sitting on the ground.'

'If that's what he did, what would he have done with the lid? There was no sign of it being dropped here,' Mike said.

'I can imagine him tossing the cap away if he was in a hurry . . . but if he thought he had all the time in the world he might have kept it and disposed of it later,' Jeff responded.

'Hmm . . . More like he tossed it I think,' Barry said. 'If he was going to take the trouble of keeping it, to dispose of it later, why wouldn't he do the same with the can?'

'Well, he didn't leave the can here, Barry. I found it just over there,' Mike said, pointing towards a group of manuka trees.

'Right, so if he did toss the cap, we have two likely places to search. Firstly, a radius around this spot here and, secondly, a radius around the spot where the can was found. How far do you think he could have thrown the cap?'

'It's a pretty lightweight plastic cap, so I wouldn't think any more than twenty metres,' Jeff suggested.

'OK, let's do a thorough search out to twenty-four metres in each case. If both searches draw a blank we'll have to start looking further afield. Mike, have you got a stake and some rope we can use? I want to put a stake at the central point and tie the rope to it. We can then measure out twenty-four metres and we'll all hold onto the rope as we travel around the circle looking. One of us can be out at the twenty-four metre mark and the other two at, say, eighteen metres and ten metres. We'll go slowly around the circle and turn over any plant material, or anything else we run into, to make sure we don't miss anything.'

The first search turned up nothing of interest.

'Damn!' Barry exclaimed. 'I had hoped I would be right about McCann tossing the cap from this position by the cabin. Searching amongst the manuka trees is going to be a lot more difficult, because of all the extra vegetation there.'

'Perhaps we should search a wider circle over there, boss,' Jeff suggested.

'Why's that?'

'I think he might have been waiting by those trees to see what would happen after he set the fire. He probably wiped the can to remove his prints whilst he was there. If he decided to toss the cap away from there, where would he have thrown it?'

'Into the thickest part of the vegetation, I'd guess,' Mike said.

'Maybe,' Jeff replied. 'But, if he wanted to toss it as far as possible, he could have thrown it off to the side . . . towards all that flax, for example.'

'I see what you are getting at, Jeff,' Barry said. 'How about we search thirty metres out from the trees, and then, say, twenty in amongst them?'

'Let's do it,' Mike said.

Forty minutes later Jeff, who was on the rope at the thirty metre mark, let out a yell.

'Yee haar! There it is! In the middle of that flax bush,' Jeff proclaimed triumphantly.

'OK, Hercule Poirot,' Barry said with a grin. 'You were right about increasing the search diameter. That cap is fully thirty metres from where the can was found. All credit to you . . . and I'm really glad we don't have to go into all that undergrowth under the trees!'

'Now all we have to hope for is that McCann didn't wipe the cap clean,' Mike said.

'Only too true, Mike. We're no further ahead if McCann's prints aren't on it, but I can tell you if there are any prints pretty quickly. I brought the gear with me.'

Jeff put on a latex rubber glove, carefully retrieved the cap from the flax bush, and placed it into a clear plastic evidence bag before handing it to his boss. Back at his car Barry took out a suitcase containing his fingerprinting gear.

'OK if I do this on the table in your caravan, Mike?'

'Sure. Go ahead.'

A few minutes later Barry looked up at Jeff and asked, 'What do you make of that, Jeff?'

'A print for sure, boss . . . but maybe not a fingerprint.'

'I agree. I think we might have a palm print. That would make sense if he had to press down to release the lock so he could unscrew it. The Motueka boys will have taken his palm prints as well as his finger prints, so we'll soon know if we've nailed our man . . . But, right now, I'm guessing we just might have a result!'

'Great work! I'm going to be crossing my fingers that the palm print belongs to McCann. I want to see him put away for a long time!' Mike exclaimed.

CHAPTER 29.

The Nelson Mail

Alleged drug dealer to face further charges

Tasman Police District Commander, Joel Hendry, today confirmed that Kenneth McCann, aged 35 years of Motueka, who has already been charged with the cultivation of cannabis for supply and has been denied bail pending his trial, now faces a charge of arson and additional charges relating to cannabis growing, processing and supply.

It is alleged that McCann burnt down a holiday home in Puponga on 27th October, after its owner reported his Puponga cannabis operation to the Police. The Mail also understands that a former associate of McCann has agreed to testify that McCann has master-minded cannabis growing operations in a number of hidden locations around the Tasman region, and the processing and sale of cannabis over the past few years.

'Shutting down a number of cannabis plantations, a processing operation and a supply network will have a major impact on the drug scene in our region,' Commander Hendry said. 'Thanks to assistance from the public and a coordinated policing effort, involving CIB detectives and uniformed police from Motueka and Takaka, we have severely curtailed the supply of illicit drugs in the Tasman district.'

The Mail understands further arrests are pending. McCann's trial is scheduled to commence on 17 December at the High Court in Nelson.

'Hey Mereana! Have you read Saturday's paper? McCann is definitely being charged with arson and he is going on trial before Christmas!'

'Let's have a look, Mike!'

Having read the article Mereana gave Mike a quick kiss on the cheek.

'It's just what we hoped for, Mike. I'm a bit surprised someone is prepared to spill the beans about his operations, but I suppose some deal has been made with whoever it is.'

'I'm sure you are right, but I'm really pleased!'

'Me too, Mike, but I'm rather surprised you haven't been told about the date for the trial, seeing you are going to be called as a witness.'

'I find that surprising too. You'd have thought that Barry Sanders would have been in touch about that . . . Mind you, he may have tried. I haven't checked my cell phone for a day or two. I better check to see if there's any message.'

'There's been nothing on my phone, Mike.'

'I'd better go and check, I think.'

Mike crossed the road and walked out onto the beach before he turned his cell phone on and heard the signal for a message received. It turned out to be from Barry Sanders and he was asking Mike to ring him. The message was dated two days previously.

'Mike Robinson here, Barry. I have only just received your message. I presume you wanted to talk about McCann's trial? I have just read about it in Saturday's paper . . . . Yes, Mereana and I are really thrilled with it all. Well done to you and all the team! . . . It sounds like it has developed into a very big deal! . . . Well I guess we started it all off, Barry, but it was you guys who got a successful outcome . . . . OK, I'll wait to hear when the pre-trial meeting is going to be . . . . OK . . . . Thanks, Barry. Catch you later then . . . Bye!'

Back in the caravan Mike said, 'There *was* a message from Barry and I've just spoken to him. Apparently the McCann case is being seen as a major result and everyone involved is still buzzing about it. I am going to be asked to have a meeting with the Crown Prosecutor in a couple of week's time.'

'Well, I think the Police deserve all the credit they can get, Mike . . . Can we talk about the house now? I think we need to work out what furniture we need to buy. If we are going to be moving in before Christmas we'll have to start doing some shopping and I see, in the paper, that some of the furniture stores are having sales at present.'

'I can tell you are going to enjoy this, Mereana!'

'What girl doesn't enjoy shopping? But we'll need to look together. Can you come back to Nelson with me on Monday morning? I think we'll need to look around a bit. It might take us two or three days to decide what we want and where to buy it.'

'All right . . . Actually, I *have* been looking forward to this. How about you make a list of what we'll need to look for? . . . Whilst I'm in Nelson I'll take some time to visit a couple of building firms and ask them to quote on having our chalets pre-fabricated, so we can just drop them in place once we have prepared the foundations.'

'Can that be done, Mike? I'd have thought the chalets would be too big to transport over the Takaka hill.'

'They shouldn't be. They're no bigger than some of the larger trucks that drive over every day.'

'That would save a lot of time then, wouldn't it?'

'Yes . . . and cost! That's why I'm considering doing it this way. All the chalets will have the same design, so it should be possible to get a good price for eleven of them. If we were thinking about having them built on site, one at a time, it would definitely take a lot longer, and the cost would be higher too because the builders would have to come over here and be put up somewhere whilst they were working on site. The way I'm proposing it's done makes it possible for the chalets to be built in the builder's workshop. As far as I can see they'll be able to do everything there, even hang the doors, lay the carpet, install the electrics and plumbing, and so on. I'm hoping the chalets can just be dropped onto their foundations and then be connected up to the wiring and pipe-work that will already be in position.'

'Wow! It sounds like we could be in business quite quickly!'

'The chalets shouldn't take all that long to prefabricate, but the central block is a different matter. That will definitely need to be built in situ. I'm hoping to find a good local builder who can do that job. Even so, I'm thinking it might take four to five months to complete the work.'

'We could start hiring out the chalets without having the main block finished, though, couldn't we?'

'I think so. We'd probably be limited to sightseers until the central block is ready. We won't be able to do any of our workshops before then.'

'It's starting to all come together now, isn't it . . .'

'Yup! We'll be fully operational in six months time I reckon. In the meantime there's quite a bit of finishing work to do on the house, but I'm sure that won't take too long. It's only things like external painting and staining, and lining out the basement. I want to have the driveway properly formed and sealed too.'

'There's not going to be much spare time then is there!'

'No, but it's going to be great when we finish it all and we can enjoy what we have achieved.'

'You have certainly done *really* well, Mike. I can't wait to see what Matiu makes of the house when he gets here for his December break . . . He's been asking about it and I've told him we are going to moving be in before Christmas.'

'Is it going to be OK for Huia and Matiu to share the second bedroom, Mereana?'

'It's not ideal, but it wouldn't be for more than a week or two, so it's not a big problem. Anyway it may not happen. Huia has already put in her request to be allowed to use the caravan when she is over here. Do you think we can agree to that, Mike?'

'I don't have any problem with it, if that's what she wants. I can understand her thinking the caravan will give her some sense of independence. But if your parents decide to visit when Matiu is here she might have to move into the house for a few days.'

'That's OK then . . . and, by the sound of it, it won't be too long before we'll have a chalet Mum and Dad can use.'

CHAPTER 30.

Six months later

Mereana and Mike invited thirty people to attend the official opening of Korimako Lodge and their wedding, a two-day event. Matiu had made the trip from Hawaii and Sarah and Paul had come from England. Mereana's parents, Jenny and George, Pastor Hone Ratahi and most of the kaumatuas from the marae were in attendance, along with a number of Mereana and Mike's long-time friends. Everyone was accommodated, twenty of them in the chalets, and the rest in the house and caravan. Caterers had been engaged to provide food and drink over the two days.

The first day was for the opening of the lodge. This was held in the amenities block, where sliding wall panels between the lounge and meeting room had been opened up to provide one large space. Hone Ratahi, acting as master of ceremonies, welcomed everyone and then acknowledged the ancestors, those who had previously lived in the area. He spoke firstly in Maori and then in English. That done, he spoke about the development of the lodge. He made special mention of its purpose as a place for language and cultural education, and for artistic endeavour. He also pointed out that people staying at the lodge would be able to explore and investigate the history of the area and enjoy the local fauna and flora. He then said a karakia, praying for the success of the new venture, and finished with a blessing for all those present. It was then Mike's turn to speak.

'Tena koutou katoa. Thank you, Hone, for acknowledging what a special place this is, both historically and at present, and for the prayers and blessings. Mereana and I would like to add our welcome and thank you all for making the trip out here today to celebrate the official opening of Korimako Lodge . . . and, tomorrow, our wedding. We especially want to acknowledge Matiu, Paul, and Julia, who have travelled across the world to be here. This means a great deal to us. We hope you will all thoroughly enjoy two days of relaxation and celebration.

'Today I'll talk mainly about Korimako Lodge. As you all know, I moved over here after my wife Rosie died. It was a difficult time and I was trying to find a way to move on with my life. I decided to build a house here and I was underway with that when Mereana turned up next door. She was staying in a cabin only metres from where we are right now. We met as neighbours, but then formed a friendship that quickly became a relationship . . . and you know that this has now developed to the stage when we are to be married tomorrow. The point is that we were both looking to our futures. What did we want to do, now that we were both on our own? It didn't take us long to realise we had fallen in love with each other, and then we discovered we also shared a love for Puponga . . . Even though it is such a tiny isolated place it has many of the things we hold dear. It has history, beauty and wildlife, and it is so peaceful here. We think it's an ideal place to explore our respective passions for writing and art. Then we hit on the idea of creating a lodge where others could share and appreciate all this. The lodge is able to be used for a variety of activities, but it was principally designed as a place where people can come to practice and maybe advance their knowledge or skills, especially with Maori language and culture, or with creative writing, which are Mereana's fortes, or as a place to create works of art and record the wonderful scenery, bird and animal life of the area, which is my own area of interest.

'You'll see that we have designed the chalets to work as self-catering units, but we also have this central amenities block to cater for groups who want to do things communally. I'm pleased to say we already have a number of bookings that are going to keep us very busy in the coming months.

'Mereana and I particularly want to thank Annabelle, who is with us today, for allowing us to buy her land, so that we could combine two properties to provide enough space to make all this work.

'Some of you will have heard that we have had some drama along the way. Mereana had to deal with the loss of her husband, Tamati, and then take over the work he was doing to prepare the Wakatu-Mohua Claim. This was an enormous task, but I'm pleased to say that the Waitangi Tribunal found all the key parts of the claim substantially proven and Mereana and all the claimants are now waiting to see what settlement is going to be offered . . . And we also had trouble with some drug dealers who were growing their cannabis out here. They took exception to us reporting their operations to the Police and exacted their revenge by completely wrecking Mereana's car and by burning down the cabin we were living in at that time. But we were not deterred and, thankfully, the culprits are now spending their days in prison . . . As far as building the lodge is concerned I have to say we had a relatively smooth run. We had excellent contractors working on the job and, by and large, things have run to schedule. It has been a very exciting period in our lives and we have seen our dreams turn into reality. We are very proud of the end result and, provided we can continue to attract enough customers to pay the bills, we will continue to be very happy.

'So thank you all again for coming to share this special day with us! Now, I'd like Mereana to stand with me . . . thank you, Mereana . . . as together we declare Korimako Lodge officially open!'

There was a prolonged burst of applause as Mike kissed Mereana and they both sat down.

'That was very well said, Mike,' Mereana whispered.

Hone Ratahi then stood to say Grace and invited everyone to partake of the buffet lunch provided.

* * * * *

After lunch many of the guests took the opportunity to wander around the grounds and along the beach. Mike looked for Matiu and found him talking to Henare Whataroa.

'Hey you two! Interested in a guided tour by any chance?'

Matiu and Henare were both delighted to be asked and Mike started by leading the way up the hill towards the back of the property. As they walked he explained how he had planned for each chalet to be located at a reasonable distance from the next and for them all to have a view across the bay. He explained that he had been able to do this without having to fell any of the large trees. In fact, he wanted each chalet to be framed by trees and for the pathways, leading from each chalet to the amenities block and car park, to meander between the trees.

'I hired a digger to remove all the topsoil where these paths are and then used it to backfill with base-course, before applying a layer of this white stone chip that you see now. It all comes from a quarry just out of Collingwood.'

'I noticed that you have named each chalet after a native bird, Mike,' Henare said. 'I am in Kereru and I see you have hung a painting of two kereru above the bed-head. That is a nice touch I think.'

'That was Mereana's suggestion, but I think it's going to keep me busy. The painting you mentioned is the second one I've done for that chalet. Some people stayed there about six weeks back and asked to buy the first painting. The same thing happened when people stayed in Tui and Kotuku!'

'It's a great way to display and sell your work, Mike. I'm sure you'll sell a lot more!' Henare exclaimed.

'I like how each chalet has a small deck, so people can sit outside if the weather is fine,' Matiu said.

'Yes, well the chalets aren't all that big really and the deck provides a bit more space . . . and it's nice to be able to look out over the bay too . . . Now, here you'll see that we have created an area where people can have a barbeque. It's a sheltered spot and there are enough chairs and tables for about twenty people. The barbeque itself is long enough to allow more than one group to be cooking at the same time . . . And just a little further up into these trees you'll see another little feature. It's a bird feeding station and a hide with one-way glass, so people can watch the birds feeding and drinking without disturbing them. You'd be amazed how many birds use it! I've seen up to twenty birds there at one time, especially silvereyes, and it seems as though different species like to come at different times of the day.'

'Wow! I really like this, Mike,' Matiu exclaimed. 'Look! There are quite a few silvereyes and some blackbirds there now! The blackbirds certainly like those apples you have cut in half for them.'

'Yes they do, but the best thing is that you can be so close to the birds . . . and it's fascinating to just sit and watch them . . . Now come along a bit further and you'll see our *piece de resistance*! . . . There you go . . . our lookout!'

They all climbed up the ladder and into the lookout.

'The views from up here are amazing, Mike!' Matiu exclaimed. 'You can see in all directions!'

'I can appreciate why you love this place so much,' Henare said. 'It truly is special . . . I can't help thinking about the Maori who lived here so long ago. It would have been a wonderful place for them back then. Everything they needed would have been right here . . .'

'I think you are right, Henare. From what Mereana tells me, it is a place that different peoples have coveted at various times over the centuries and, unfortunately, because of that it has been fought over and people have been killed, or enslaved, or displaced . . . and then, more recently, it was sold for a pittance to the colonialists who saw potential for farming and mining.'

'It's sad that we human beings have always tried to take what we want by force, or trickery, Mike. It doesn't seem to matter what race of people we are, we have all been prepared to do this.'

'Do you not think we live in more enlightened times now, though, Henare?' Mike asked.

'I'd like to think so, but our history would suggest that we may eventually see a repeat of the cycle of injustice. Who knows? In the meantime you should enjoy what you have here. You have certainly created something you can be very proud of and I particularly like the fact that you are offering others the chance to share the experience. You are not just keeping it all for yourselves.'

'Well we do have to charge something to cover our costs, but apart from that . . . yes . . . we do want to share it.'

'I can tell Mum is as proud of all this as you are, Mike. She is one very happy lady! I want you to know that Huia and I really appreciate how much you have contributed to that.'

Mike felt a surge of emotion and felt a familiar tightening in his throat, but he was able to whisper, 'Thank you Matiu,' as he shook the young man by the hand. Henare looked on with a broad smile on his face and nodded his approval.

* * * * *

The wedding took place in the lodge at 11.00am the next morning. Mereana had two bridesmaids, Huia and Julia. Mike had Paul as his best man and Matiu as his groomsman. Mereana looked stunning in a full-length sleeveless dress made of peach-coloured satin, with matching shoes. Her hair was drawn back to cascade down her back, highlighting her facial features and the greenstone pendant she wore around her neck. Huia and Julia had matching mid-length satin dresses, azure blue in colour, with matching blue shoes. The men wore navy-blue suits with pale blue shirts, open at the collar.

The guests were all pre-seated at their tables when George Parata escorted Mereana into the room, with the two bridesmaids following behind. He led them up to the front of the room where Mike, Paul and Matiu waited to one side of Pastor Ratahi. The sliding windows across the entire front of the room had been drawn right back to provide an unobstructed view across the bay. Against this backdrop Hone Ratahi stepped up to a lectern and began the ceremony.

The wedding was traditional in style, with the usual vows and exchange of rings, and there were two hymns, one sung in English and the other in Maori. A photographer took a combination of snapshots and video coverage of the proceedings. At the end of the ceremony, after Hone Ratahi had declared that they were now husband and wife, a smiling Mike and Mereana kissed each other and then turned to face the seated guests.

'Ladies and Gentlemen, I present to you . . . Mr and Mrs Robinson!' Hone cried.

This was greeting by loud applause and everyone rose to their feet and continued clapping as the bridal party moved to their table and sat down.

The tables were set for a banquet and, after Hone had said Grace, the first course was served and red and white wine was delivered to the tables.

The speeches were made at the end of the first course and everyone was asked to charge their glasses in readiness for the toasts. George Parata did a sterling job as Master of Ceremonies and, after the toasts to absent friends, to the bride's parents, and to the bridesmaids, he called on Henare Whataroa to propose the toast to the bride and groom. Henare kept his speech short, but he made it very clear that he was genuinely delighted to have been asked to propose this particular toast. Every stood to drink to 'the bride and groom' and then Mike was called upon to reply.

'Tena koutou katoa. Kia ora, Henare. Thank you for your kind words and for proposing the toast to Mereana and myself . . . To you all, I would like to say it means a great deal that you are all here with Mereana and I today, to see us demonstrate our love for each other by entering into marriage. We would like to thank you for coming and for your wonderful wedding gifts. We are so privileged to receive them and they are truly appreciated . . . So thank you again . . . I am going to keep this speech quite short, because Mereana also wants to speak, but I must say how honoured and privileged I feel to have Mereana as my wife. Sometimes I find it difficult to believe how lucky I am. I am truly blessed and I will be doing my utmost to ensure she always remains as happy as she obviously is today . . . I feel this is a fantastic occasion, not just because our families are here, but because our dearest friends are here also. Mereana and I will always treasure this day . . . Now, I'll hand over to Mereana.'

'Kia ora, Mike, and ki a koutou katoa. It has been really wonderful that you have all been able to join Mike and I for two days and, for most of you, two nights as well . . . firstly to be present at the opening of Korimako Lodge yesterday and, secondly, to witness our wedding today. You have helped us celebrate two beginnings . . . the beginning of Korimako Lodge . . . and the start of our married life together. I must say I am looking forward to both with huge anticipation and excitement. Mike said he felt honoured that I was prepared to become his wife . . . Well, I think it is me that should feel honoured! And I don't think he needs to worry about doing anything more to ensure I remain happy! He just needs to continue to be the caring, wise soul-mate that he is. Mike's empathy and friendly nature is probably what has made it so easy for our respective families to come together, with genuine affection, as a new extended family . . . And I am very proud of what Mike has achieved here in Puponga. He has built our new house, almost single-handedly, and he has designed and managed the complete development of Korimako Lodge. It was his idea to create this place and I think what he has achieved is remarkable . . . I want to thank you, Paul, and you, Matiu, for standing by Mike today. I know he was proud to ask you to be his Best Man and Groomsman . . . And I want to thank Julia and Huia for being my bridesmaids . . . Thank you so much . . . and not just for today, but for all the help you have given me in the lead-up to the wedding as well . . . Finally, I want to say that Mike and I hope you will all take the opportunity to come back to see us in future and take some time to enjoy what Puponga has to offer. You will be most welcome. All you need to do is give us a call, to make sure we have accommodation available when you are able to come. I hope you all enjoy the rest of the meal and the rest of the celebrations this afternoon and through into the evening. E noho ra . . . Noho rangimairie . . .'

As Mereana sat down there was loud applause and spontaneous calls of 'kia ora' and 'ka pai'. She leaned towards Mike and whispered, 'How did I do, Mike?'

'Perfect! But then, I'd expect a school-teacher to be able to capture the audience,' he said with a grin.

George Parata then rose to speak again.

'Ladies and Gentlemen . . . The main course is about to be served and then, for those who would like dessert, a dessert buffet will be set up at the back of the room . . . Just help yourself . . . During the rest of the afternoon you'll have plenty of time to mix and mingle, and later on we will have a DJ here. I hope you'll sing along and, once we have cleared away the tables, you'll be able to do some dancing too!'

* * * * *

It was after midnight when Mereana and Mike made it to bed.

'Phew, Mike! I'm feeling a bit tipsy! It's been such a wonderful day and everyone has been so nice. I'm still buzzing with it all . . . I don't think I'm going to be able to sleep just yet.'

'No? Well, maybe we could contemplate doing something else for a while. I'm still wide awake myself!'

'What did you have in mind?'

'I'll give you one guess . . . It's something very personal, very intimate, and very pleasurable . . . and it often happens in bed . . .'

'I can't possibly guess, Mike . . . I think you'll have to show me . . .'

'I think I can manage that, Mereana . . .'

BIBLIOGRAPHY

Brailsford, Barry. 1981—The Tattooed Land—The Southern Frontiers of the Pa Maori. AH & AW Reed

Department of Conservation—*www.doc.govt.nz*

Dwyer, Peter. 2003—Coal Mines of Puponga. October Enterprises t/a River Press

Mitchell, Hilary and John. 2004—Te Tau Ihu O Te Waka—A history of Maori of Nelson and Marlborough. Huia Publishers

New Zealand Birds—*www.nzbirds.com*

Petit, Chris. 1999—Farewell Spit—A changing landscape. Terracottage Books

Te Ara Encyclopedia of New Zealand—*www.teara.govt.nz*

The Tangata Whenua Tribes of Te Tau Ihu—*www.theprow.org.nz*

Waitangi Tribunal Reports—*www.waitangi-tribunal.govt.nz*

AUTHOR'S NOTE

None of the modern day characters in this book is a real person, nor are they based on any particular person. I have drawn on my personal experience with people generally and have used imagination to create my characters.

The events described in this book, involving the main characters, are all fictitious. However, the locations mentioned do exist and much of the history referred to in Korimako did happen.

The Waimea Marae and the Waimea Corporation do not exist and they should not be compared, in any way, to any actual marae, or corporation. Similarly the Wakatu-Mohua Claim, as described in this book, is fictitious and should not be compared with any actual claim before the Waitangi Tribunal, or Office of Treaty Settlements.

Special thanks to my wife, Glen, who read my early drafts and gave constructive criticism and support. Thanks also to retired Sergeant Graeme Wilkes who provided valuable guidance on policing matters.

Another book by

David Nelson

The Herons Return

After the death of his wife in Europe Jamie Jordon returns to New Zealand to discover his grandparent's apple orchard has become an abandoned quarry. The laid-to-waste landscape is a disgrace that Jamie vows to remedy.

Hard-nosed businessman, Terry McKechnie, is responsible for this environmental vandalism. He and Jamie's ex-girlfriend, Liz Lawrence, have a marriage of convenience, but Terry wants more and becomes violent when Liz refuses.

Jamie decides to restore the worked-out quarry and turn it into a top-class resort and country club, and when Liz leaves Terry he offers her employment. Suspecting the pair have become more than work colleagues, Terry's drunken retaliation backfires and Liz's hopes for a better life are shattered.

Lightning Source UK Ltd.
Milton Keynes UK
UKOW04f0624260116

267073UK00002B/301/P

9 781456 813345